Acknowledgem...

I always say, I never ch... author chose me. I think in some ways I did choose this lifestyle. Because it's been seven years since I published my first book. And I haven't quit yet. I want to thank my family. Especially my brother's Zully and Cadence. They never let me go through anything alone. I want to thank my crew. They know who they are. I'll say their names anyway. My bff's Noel aka Mystery Woman Music, Tiffany Cole, Kendra, Corey B Music, Queen Roxxy(Rip), Kova, Dante, Tara a professional masseuse. And last but not least, my best friend Warren Stewart aka Dj Hypnotic who has been there from the start. I love you all past the YOUniverse. I can say. Because we're all spiritual people. Ase!!

P.s Follow Them On IG

@Mysterywomanmusic @Coreybmusic
@Dsf_kingzully @Officiallycadence @Nutella.g0d
@Queennation_bytiffany @Djhypnotic

Prolouge 1966

EXT. Bahamas- Night

This was no ordinary night for nineteen year old street king, Jesse Jean, and his ride or die as the hood calls it, accomplice Elliana Jones. Also his longtime girlfriend, and now fiance. Celebrating their rise to ghetto fame as Southside Chicago's best crack connect, Jesse Jean and Elliana matched each other's fly. Jesse's high cheek bones brought a statue-like structure to his copper brown face. His curvy lips were sexy, fully melanated as if the sun kissed them every night before he went to bed. His dark brows met right across from one another, one being more arched. He rocked a fresh temp fade, two French braids cornrowed tight into his scalp. Casually dressed in white ripped capris, a yellow Hollister t-shirt, and a denim Jean vest. A steel pole held him up by his forearm. His bottle of PERRIER JOUET BELLE EPOQUE, 2012 in one hand. A pistol in the other. Elliana stood beside him in a red mini dress. Her natural curls pinned up into a Mohawk, the gold eyeshadow darkening her already cinnamon brown eyes. She raised her glass, toasting to her man's success. Jesse gulped his drink, but wasn't at all satisfied. There was thirty five thousand dollars of his money missing, and he intended to find out where it went.

Chapter #1

EXT: Early Morning

Strapped to the pole of Jesse Jeans high-class prom bateau, drenched in blood, getting his teeth swiped out from his gums, Ayinda craved for his life as Jesse gave him double knuckle sandwiches to his jaw.
  "Fuck is my money at Ayinda?" Jesse strikes his face, slashing his cheek open.

Ayinda howled at the screeching noise of his skin tearing as if it were a sheet of white paper being shredded in half. "You know damn well, I don't play about my green."
 Jesse said, clenching his jaws together, holding a knife up to Ayinda's adam's apple.
 "Start fucking talking."
Adjacent of where they were, Elliana had Ayinda's baby mom Essence, held at gunpoint.
 "Jesse stop." She pleaded. "I'll tell you where the fucking money is." She wept. Pressed for Ayinda to leave word where and what they did with Jesse's drugs and money, Essence let it slip that they were set up by the police in exchange for vital information on Jesse's drug operations, and the Italian Alessandro mafia family. Elliana read Jesse's face like a Dr. Seuss book. He didn't have to say a word. Elliana tightened her grip, clutching Essence by her throat.
 "Say the word babe." She says snagging Essence at the neck.
 "You grimey bitch." Ayinda bedeviled.
 He smirks, spitting out his teeth, which rolled across the dock like a set of dice. "Elliana, baby girl." He gapes at her, blood spilling from his lips. "Kill that hoe all you want."   His dying laugh echoed over top of the sea.
 "She thinks I don't know--" He cracked his
last smile, "That she fucked Jesse."
A lump breeded in Essence's throat. Furthermore, the waves of the water were making her seasick. Suddenly she wanted to vomit.
 "Elliana wait." She gulped, swallowing her spit. "It wasn't like that."
 She began defining the events of that night between her and Jesse. "We were drunk." She stuttered.
 A tear at a time slid down her golden cheeks.

"One thing led to another." She interpreted, mourning the animalistic behavior that had taken place with them.
"Babe."
Elliana's eyes instantly water, the static in her head, electrifying every part of her brain. Her stomach felt empty.
"You fucked Essence?" She asked, now displaying her pistol in Jesse's face as the tears streamed down her cheeks.
Sobbing against her chest, Jesse clutched her waist apologizing. Elliana pulled away from him nearly collapsing on the dock of the boat. The painful thought of Jesse sleeping with Essence hit her every single second. As much as she wanted to hold back her tears, the noise of her hysterical cries came from deep within her throat. The taste in her mouth is as salty as the water they're sailing on. The smell of fish caused her to feel nauseous.
Ayinda stared directly at his dirty lover. "The streets talk Essence."
Ayinda's eyes told Essence, she should have known he knew the truth about her and Jesse.
"You're a greasy, unfaithful whore."

Elliana blacked out, smacking the shit out of Essence with the butt of her pistol. She yanked her by her ponytail, dragging her toward the railing of the boat. Essence kicked her feet screaming, "Elliana no. I'm sorry. Jesse couldn't lock horns with the unhappy wound he brought into him and Elliana's relationship. She warned him long ago; that she'd kill a bitch in a heartbeat if she ever espied that he slept around on her. Meanwhile Essence is throwing a temper tantrum.   "Fuck You Ayinda." She screamed. "Fuck you nigga."
"Sad."

Elliana hysterically cried. "We're only eighteen." She sniffles, wiping her eyes with the palm of her hand.

"You had your entire life ahead of you." She shrugged. "Until now."

Her eyes fell to no remorse. She glanced at Jesse one last time. His mouth was as dry as a cactus. Elliana giggles insanely beneath her breath.

"Jesse Jean is mine." She says, pressing the barrel of her gun against Essence's temple.

"And mine only."

Elliana put her finger on the trigger, squeezing it, airing the clip out on Essence as the yacht sailed into the foggy night. She set fire to Jesse, unimaginable cramps in her eyes.

"We're done." She snivels, tossing the evidence into the water. Her eight inch heels clacked against the floor of the yacht as she walked away, leaving Jesse to break up with Ayinda.

****

EXT. Thursday 7PM- November 26th- 40+ yrs later

The day before Thanksgiving, shots rang out in one of the most dangerous neighborhoods of Southside Chicago, Fuller Park, a single family block now, notoriously known for gangs and drugs. Also the same street that Cashmere, and his grandmother Elliana Jean lived on. The outcry of bullets hardly phased either of them anymore. However, this incident disturbed them. Fuller Park, known as the slums for gangs, such as the Cobras, Dynamites, and the absolute worst one, Cut Throat. Most nights Elliana Jean worried herself to death; that one day it'd be Cashmere's body lying in the swing of his own blood. She holds his hand for dear life, her eyes saddened at the mother, who

screamed for her son to breathe until the ambulance came. Her racket of cries hit Elliana Jeans ears in a way that she would never lose consciousness of. Cashmere's pager alerted him to reply to a message. He retrieves the black device from his hip. The person paging him was his godbrother Marco. He clicks on the number. Marco immediately picks up on the first ring.
 "Sup homie?" He checks in.

Cashmere sees his acquaintance Pee-Wee on the ground, fighting for his life. His mother is literally pulling her micro braids out, yelling. "Breathe baby. Breathe." She's rocking him against her chest, howling, and praying. "God don't take my baby." Pee-Wee began to drift away. His liveliness had gone far away from him. The saliva in his mother's mouth thickened as she swallowed her spit. Her eyes are full of fear. She wanted to run somewhere safe. Instead she stayed where she was, cradling her child's dead body.
 Cashmere stood to his feet. Elliana Jean locks his hand in hers. He kissed her forehead.
 "I'm good NaNa. Let me holla at Marco."
 Marco was close by. He came walking up the block, meeting Cashmere at the bottom of the stoop. He whispers, keeping the conversation between the two of them.
 "Fuck happened dawg."
 "Pigs is tweaking out here bruh." Cashmere uttered. "They hit Pee-Wee's head bruh."
 Marco's level of anger hit the roof. His demeanor went from calm to wanting to body a nigga. Any nigga at that. Cops, haters, whoever. Pee Wee was the coolest kid ever. Always laughing and shit. Definitely a mommas boy. Cashmere recalled the first time Pee Wee told him his mother would buy him a car for his sixteenth birthday, but

he had to make the honor roll. The boy was as smart as Einstein. On a spring day last summer, Pee Wee rolled up on the block in a champagne, Honda accord. He hollered out the driver side "look at cha boy" with a big kool aid smile on his dark chocolate face. Reminiscing on that day, Marco sighed.

"Out of all niggas." He shook his head, disappointed. "Ma fuckin Pee-Wee though."

Cashmere, and Marco kept their conversation at an arm's length, but were thinking the exact same thing. They sat up on the porch, plotting to loot whatever evidence the police confiscated out of Pee-Wee's car. It would take a good ten minutes for them to walk around the corner to Kedzie Avenue, pop the trunk of the cop car, snatch the jewels, money, and what little bit of weed he had. The narcotics, they would sell to the bigger dealers for a percentage. Hell that's what the cops do anyway. There's never a middle situation. You're either a good cop or a crooked cop. Adrenaline pumped in Cashmere's veins as they peeped a detective in a three piece cool grey suit and handed his colleague a zip lock bag with a debit card in it, another one with chains, and a few hundred dollar bills.

"Look, look, look." Marco pressured Cashmere pulling on his arm. "He's taking that bag to the whip on the ave."

"So what are we waiting on? Let's go get it." Cashmere insisted. "NaNa." He says, "I'll be right back."

(Music Playing)

*For the
nigga
that
killed my*

homie
(woo)
Make sure he die slow.

(Slow Motion)
   Cashmere and Marco parade up Kedzie Avenue, hiding their identities behind a pair of black masks. Their feet barely touching the ground as they sought out to complete their mission. They dip midway up a pissy alleyway. Their eyes glued to the cops every move. It only took a few seconds for him to toss the bags in the back. He communicates through his walkie talkie to his captain that everything was clear, that he was on his way back to the crime scene. As soon as the cop turned his back, Marco aimed straight for his head.
  (Slow Motion) (Music Playing)

I know a killer that's ready to shoot something.
   In a moment's time, the body of the man in his blue crooked uniform fell to the ground.
(Music Playing)
But he shoots with his eyes closed
Better watch how you speak on that OTF shit.
   Marco and Cashmere rushed the vehicle, popping the trunk using a crowbar taking every bit of information there was. (Music Playing)
'Cause shit, I'd die for it
I'll go against the grain for one of my niggas
Shit, if I got to
If I got to, boom, boom, boom, boom

   The plan went as smooth as butter. Cashmere was robbing society with greed and malice. Him and Marco wanted revenge served to the streets on a platter of ice for the death of their homie Pee-wee. Cashmere guarded the scenery, while Marco took everything in sight, sentimental as well as valuable. It has been this way for him since he was a kid, love turns into hate; and in his own fucked up thoughts, he felt secure doing the cops just as dirty as they did everyone else.

This was the life he was born into, raised with, this was the world he knew.

Him and Cashmere both fled to the corner of the alley, where puddles of water soaked the ground, getting their sneakers wet. Dark clouds gave off thick raindrops as they ran toward a set of rusted fire escapes leading to second floor apartments. While footing it to someplace safe a bag of money slipped through Cashmere's hands. He slid through the mud, unclean water splashing against his lips. Forcing himself not to fall, he uncovered his eyes from the rain.

"Shit."

He murmured running along. He almost lost his cool, but hurried to retrieve the bag and keep it pushing.

"Bruh you good?" Marco says, giving a hand to get Cashmere on his feet.

"I'm good bruh. I'm good. Let's get the fuck from around here."

Their ol head Paco lived in the apartment with the plexiglass on it. No one could see in, but he could see out. He was home sitting on his sofa smoking an L for Pee-Wee when Cashmere and Marco came flying up the fire escape to his window. Cashmere glares over his shoulder, perspiring from running. Cop cars surrounded Kedzie Avenue from one end of the block to the next. Their sirens sing trouble in the air. As Finley is walking toward his car, he gets a glimpse of his partner Yates lying in the street.

(Slow Motion)

Fluent in action at the same time feeling as if his feet weren't going nowhere, Finley sped off yelling his partners name.

"Yates." He bellowed out. "Yates."

He blared in operation feeling as if the ground had fallen from under him. Skinning his knees on the pavement, Finley clutched Yates in his arms. He drove his fist into Yate's chest. His eyes boiling with hitting back whoever killed his partner. Mishandling his walkie talkie, he held the button that allowed him to communicate with their captain Ruiz, a classy, caramel complexion woman from Mexico. Ruiz breathed the life of being part of the enforcement of the law. Nothing else satisfied her other than getting twisted thugs off the streets. Finley could smell the scent of her coming up behind him. Her Marc Jacobs perfume, Daisy Eau de Toilette stung his nostrils as she corresponded to him.

"Fuck." She uttered in disbelief, meeting Yates lying on the sidewalk dead.

"Yates is down." She informed the other detective.

Ruiz faced Finley with a look of mistake on her face. She kneels beside Yates whispering.
"You were a good cop. God bless your familia."

Swiping her bangs out of her eyes, she stares Finley in the eye.

"This is what we do to my officers?" She spoke in a coarse, candy-coated tone. Her cool grey pants- suit attached to her body like a chocolate covered candy bar. Her somber style accentuated with Macs black lipstick.

"We leave--" She rolls her eyes at Finley, click clacking her high heels across the pavement, "Our fucking partners.... by... their fucking self." Ruiz fiddled the

pebbles in the street with the tip of her stiletto. "Its a fucking mess out here." She spat at him. "You."
　She shouts, embarrassing Finley, pointing at him as if he were a child on the first day of school and her teacher. "Call the coroner. Talk to the witnesses. Clean this shit up." She said in a dissatisfied voice.

　　　　　********

Kedzie ave is definitely a hot spot. Paco spied the anxiety on Cashmere's face. Rather than offering him the blunt, he poured him a shot of Henny.
　"Pee-Wee was my young boi too." He said, taking a shot with him. "He ain't deserve that shit." Marco's eyes welled up with fret. Paco ran the streets for a long time. He perceived just what they were feeling, the thoughts that were executing their callow minds. "Marco give me the gun." Paco tells him, clinching the piece of steel from his hands.
　"I never thought of killing anyone till now," says Cashmere as he sat plotting on him and Marco's next move. It took almost an hour for the cops to leave the scene. Once the last car rolled out, Cashmere and Marco removed their masks, sticking them up under their shirts. Walking as if nothing happened, they stayed calm until they reached Cashmere's grandmother's front porch.
　"How you doing NaNa?" Marco greets her with a hug, and a kiss on her forehead.
　"I'm a tired baby. Real, real tired." She supports the weakness in her legs by using her cane to assist her in standing up. "I'm worried about you two," She says, wobbling to stand up straight.
　"Let me help you up." Marco lends his shoulder for her to lean on.

While Marco walked NaNa into the house, Cashmere sat thinking to himself. Chicago was his life. He couldn't pick up and move, taking his grandmother away from the only place she ever called home, but he had to do something. The heart of the city just wasn't there anymore.

Night

The love Sixteen year old Cashmere has for his grandmother is indescribable. Becoming her primary caretaker, after his grandfather Jesse passed away a year ago from pancreatic cancer meant he had to pick up the slack, and be the man of the house. There wasn't a thing Cashmere wouldn't do for his precious g-ma. After all if it wasn't for her birthing his mother Alexis, there'd be no him, so yes he catered to his grandma's every need. On Friday's he did her laundry. Throughout the week he prepped her meals. Thanks to grammy, he knew a thing or two about cooking. Cashmere could cook his ass off. Sometimes his homies Pee Wee and Paco would stop by. They knew he didn't come out to chill until his grandmother had everything she needed. That included ironing her clothes, bathing her, feeding her, and whatever else she requested. Not that Elliana was completely disabled, but here and there, uncomfortable pins and needles greeted her pre-ancient existence.

The one thing that makes Elliana the happiest is her home. For forty plus years, she resided in a red brick house that she, and her late husband Jesse Jean owned. She sat in the exact same spot everyday, where a cocoa colored, seventy two inch cordless shade kept out the cold in the winter time. Adjacent from her, a six foot artificial Hawaiian palm tree, planted in a white tower radiated the patio.

Elliana enjoyed the comfort of her personal space, the warm breeze blessing her melanated skin beneath a silk robe. Under a Cancun striped area rug, her feet are snug in a pair of therapedic, pink booty slippers.

A woman of fine decor, a blue cornered chair gave her rear end just enough cushion for her to relax. The double knitted blush throw blanket, imprinted with Elephants over her lap. On the wicker table was a People Magazine. Elliana opened the book and a picture of this year's grammy nominees popped up. BET was doing a tribute to the great Nipsey Hussle. As she is flipping through the pages reading with the one good eye she had about the slain artist, she calls her grandson outside. He gracefully answers. "Yes ma'am," joining her, sitting in the single chair across from her.

"Sup NaNa?" He propped his foot up on the table.

Every now and then Cashmere liked to tempt the old lady. He did it out of love to make her laugh. He knew good and well his grandmother adored quality furnishings.

"Boy if you don't get cho goddamn feet off my--" Cashmere laughed his butt off. "Imma kick yo ass."

"Chill NaNa." He says lacing up his brand new Air Max sneakers.

Elliana whacked him with her cane. "I know what you do when you put me to bed." She rolls her eyes. "Mr. Cashmere Jean."   She closed the magazine.

"I'm no damn fool."

She waves her cane in his face.

"I have been on this earth longer than you have been alive."

"It's not as deep as you think NaNa."

"Is that so? You and Marco wanna end up like that kid from earlier? Huh? Your mother's in jail Cashmere." Her

eyes filled with giving up ready to throw in the towel. "I sure as hell can't protect you. Hell." She sighs.
"I can barely walk or see straight."
"I'm good NaNa. I promise. And Marco is too."

INT. 1AM- Friday 11/27

A fatigued voice, eyes dead on its feet, Elliana Jean groaned in her sleep underneath a Coral king size comforter. Dreaming that Cashmere had been shot a few feet away from her, she burned herself out uttering *"No, no, no."* In her wealth of a nightmare, Cashmere is done-for. She's running toward him, but she's exasperated. Wanting to wake up out of that horrid trance, she couldn't. Sleep paralysis bound her head to the fluffy pillows. Coming back to how things were, she turned over in bed in the dark to cut the table lamp on. She flinched at the brightness blinding her groggy eyes. She's squinting, calling Cashmere's phone. Unsuccessful at seeing the digits on the keypad to dial the correct number, she throws the phone on the floor. Usually she kept her cane alongside the nightstand. This time she lost her balance getting up, stumbling to the floor. Her cheek met the cold red ceramic floor tile.

Fragile, up in age, Elliana's energy wasn't what it used to be. She crawled out to the hallway sobbing in excruciating pain. Although Cashmere wasn't in her eyesight, the smell of him lingered as he tiptoed in the house. He's walking toward the bedroom, Elliana is groaning. He runs in her direction, tripping over her arm, hitting his head on the wall. *THUMP!!* "Aahhh shit." He gasped, flicking on the hall light. His grandmother was lying there, her droopy tittie hanging out of her bra. "Fuck," he says.

Cashmere scooped his grandmother up into his arms.

"I gotchu NaNa." He said, carrying her back to bed. He laid her down on her back. "Ummm." She cried out loud sniffling as the pain of having her hip replaced rippled through her body. Cashmere got her a glass of water, and Motrin to subdue her agony. She sipped the water, swallowing the white pill until it was gone. She blinks. "You left me tonight to run the streets." She mutters. "I know you did." Cashmere sighs.

"It's not like that NaNa. Marco and I were just chilling."

You couldn't fool ol Mrs. Elliana Jean. In her younger days, she ran the streets with the baddest dope boys of Chicago making drops for them, stealing cars. That's how she met Cashmere's grandfather Jesse. A damn near wax figure of the actor, Lyric Bent. They became the dynamic duo of the city. The water doesn't run too far from the faucet. Just like Cashmere, his mother also stuck up a few kids of her own. She was found guilty by association for a murder charge at the age of eighteen and sentenced to Pontiac Corrections Prison.

INT. 3:45am- Friday

Cashmere lay on his back in his full bed staring up at the antique ceiling, distressed in beige. He thought over and over again about the kid he and Marco robbed just a few hours ago. He tossed, turning to his side. His guilty conscious fucking with him. He felt remorseful taking that kids food stamp card, and twenty dollars that most likely belonged to the mother.

(Indistinct talking)

Two black men, one named Big Lo, a six foot, three hundred pound OG were on the corner of
North Kedzie Avenue. Wondering exactly what was going on, Cashmere patrolled the perfect transaction taking

place between the two right before his half-grown eyes. He skipped from his bedroom to his grandmother's, finding her sound asleep. Assured that she was out for the count, he scurried down the steps as quietly as he could. By then Big Lo was already on the way to his ride.

EXT. Night

Cashmere approached Big Lo in what he assumed to be safe. Big Lo spun to him, a nine millimeter in his hand. Cashmere paused dead in his tracks, raising his arms above his head. He stood firm as a rock no heart in the world. Staring into the barrel of the pistol, he wondered what would happen had he taken one more step. Hardly intimidated, Cashmere peeped the tattoos on Big Lo's big round face. He wanted to ask if they were gang related but decided to stick to his original question.
 "I ain't mean to run up on you." He explained.
 "You lil broke niggas," Big Lo huffed. "It's that shit right there-- " He pulls his expensive jeans up-- "that'll get your ass put in a bodybag."
 "Wouldn't be the first time."
 Big Lo looked confused as hell. He lowered his gun, keeping it in eyesight. "Lil nigga you act like you died before." He chuckles. "Take ya lil young dumb ass in the house, and go to bed." "I saw what you did." Cashmere proceeds to keep the, not so nice conversation going. "Can you put me on?"
 Big Lo grilled Cashmere as if he were a disgusting plate of food, blatantly dismissing the question. He went on to get in his truck and go home. Chicago cops always got time for the bullshit. They'll arrest your ass just for buying a new pair of sneakers. The adrenaline in Cashmere stirred up his confidence. He sucked his teeth.

"All you have to do is say no bruh." He shrugs his shoulders in an aggravating way.

Big Lo walking and talking sarcastically says, "I did say no nigga."

"Nah." Cashmere disagreed. "You ain't say shit my nigga."

"Lil nigga," Big Lo quizzed him. "Don't get crushed out here."

"Crushed?" Cashmere laughs. "I might be sixteen, but this block knows me. Feel me?" He says, securing himself against his opponent.

Big Lo beheld a run through of Cashmere's five nine structure, marking him top to bottom. Plain as day, no tattoos, piercings, or even a whip to claim, Big Lo entertained Cashmere into taking a ride with him to his trap house. No concerns at all, Cashmere got in the front seat of Big Lo's Burgundy Suburban truck. His eyes pacified at the leather interior, tv's and tinted windows. As they're cascading over potholes, Big Lo pushed a button on his steering wheel. Money In The Grave by Drake and Rick Ross blared from the speakers.

"This my shizzy right here bruh." Cashmere nods his head. *"I mean, where the f*** should I really even start."* He went on rapping all the words, his crisp voice resoluting the lyrics, matching the energy of the song. Meanwhile Big Lo lit a fat blunt. Grey smoke clouding the roof of his truck.

"You wanna hit this?" He asked, passing the blunt.

"Nah. I don't smoke." Cashmere says, between rapping the song, rejecting, intoxicating his body. *"I got hoes that*

I'm keepin' in the dark." Big Lo's cracking up laughing, coughing on the dro going into his lungs.

(*Music Playing*)

I got my niggas 'cross the street livin' large
Thinkin' back to the fact that they dead
Thought my raps wasn't facts 'til they sat with the bars
I got two phones, one need a charge
Yeah, they twins, I could tell they ass apart
I got big packs comin' on the way
I got big stacks comin' out the safe
I got Lil Max with me, he the wave
It's a big gap between us in the game
In the next life, I'm tryna stay paid
When I die, put my money in the grave

(Music Fades)

A few turns, and green lights, Big Lo pulls up to a house that looked as if it's been sucked under water and left there four hundred years ago. The exterior of the place was so run down, Cashmere began thinking if he wanted to go inside or not. OCD, he would snap the fuck out walking in seeing shit all over the place. He made it extremely obvious that he wasn't feeling the place. Big Lo gapes at him and keeps walking.
 "You can take your little scary ass back to the truck."
 "Psh, me? Scary? Never bruh."
 "Then stop looking like a bitch and come on."
  Cashmere stayed on Big Lo's heels. The porch looked as if it were about to crumble as the two of them walked up the steps. Big Lo banged on the door. He laughed hard as

hell knowing his bodyguard Matthias would open it ready to shoot. Matthias had a voice so deep it scared you. The sound of a gun cocked. Matthias roared, "Who the fuck is it?" Big Lo chuckled until he couldn't breathe.

"It's me" man." He retorted. "Open the door. It's cold as fuck out here." Just as Big Lo predicted, Matthias cracked the door with the barrel of his pistol staring Big Lo in the face.

Cashmere got a fast glimpse of Matthias's full bearded pale skin, and sinister brown eyes.

Standing six foot six, husky, tattoos on his neck and forehead, Matthias let them in.

"This fool was really gonna kill us." Big Lo joked.

"Nah." Cashmere said, unimpressed. "He was gonna kill you. I don't have nothing to do with nothing. Feel me."
Big Lo clenched his lips together. He was fed up with Cashmere and his sarcastic mouth.

"Lighten up kid." Matthias told him.
Cashmere demands respect no matter where, or who it comes from. He gawked Matthias in the eye. His face is stone cold serious. The posture in which he stood frightening, and appealing. "Don't call me kid." He replied with a look of uncomfort. I'm a grown man in these streets." Matthias cocked his pistol.

"Okay you two." Big Lo laughs, interfering between them. The veins in Cashmere's head were bulging out. He kept cool standing there as if Matthias didn't threaten him. Finally they go inside of the house. It had no odor, however there was ass and titties everywhere. Ladies were skinned naked. Men had their dicks out. Cashmere got sick to his stomach. Everybody seemed to be cool ass naked in front of each other.

"Sup bruh."
A worker approached him.

"My name is young grip."

"Yea aight." Cashmere stepped back. "You close bruh." His fists form into a knot. "I don't like that." Grip respectively gave Cashmere seven feet of space. He didn't want no problems, or he'd have to answer to Big Lo, and Matthias.

Big Lo's main girl Maggie came out. Maggie was dark chocolate like Aunt Jemima's pancake syrup. She kept a smile on her face, friendly, but ruthless when it came to the rules of the game.

She introduced herself, shaking Cashmere's hand. He's mesmerized at how beautiful she is. Staring at her sprite shaped figure, his glossy eyes met hers. They exchanged a secret hello as if they'd end up fucking later on.

"You're here because you want in?" She smirks. "Right?" She guessed. "So what do you want?"

"What do you have?" Cashmere licks his lips.

Maggie opened the closet door closest to the electric stove. Cashmere felt his pores getting clammy. He didn't blink a lick. All he could think about was the product. The closet door closed.

Cashmere slowly came back to his senses. Maggie turns to him, a half of a smile on her face.

She tossed the bag at Cashmere. Her gorgeous smile disappeared. She became more serious. "I got it," says Cashmere.

Adina Riley 4:45am Friday

She'd seen her alcoholic father Quinn, beat on her mother Avah for the final time. The last thing she remembered is telling him to leave, never come back. Quinn choked the mother of his daughter on their bedroom floor as she wept like a scared child. Avah had been hanging up pictures she'd bought from Target earlier that day when her husband came home drunk. He hollered at her to quit banging, making all that ma-fuckin noise as she's hammering the nail in the wall to put the picture up.

Working ten hours a day packing up to sixty pound boxes at Amazon's warehouse, going to school twice a week for her GED on Mondays and Wednesdays, Avah did her best to make their deteriorating apartment a home. Quinn didn't show the least bit of appreciation. All he did was scream, holler and complain.

Early this morning, Adina came strutting home high as a kite to her parents arguing. The sound of breaking glass emanates from the upstairs bedroom. Adina recalled countless nights of her mother and father arguing. Afterwards they'd end up having sex or he'd come home with
flowers, cards and jewelry. All bought with drug money. And her mother obliged to her father's abusive ways every single time.

Going straight upstairs to her room, Adina got her towel off the bed. A nice hot shower would help get her mind right. She reached for the doorknob, the door hardly hanging onto the hinges, and the whole thing fell. *BANG!!* It hit the floor. Meanwhile Quinn and Avah are going toe to toe with each other.

"I can't take this shit no more, Quinn you have to go." Avah squealed fucking up her mascara, dodging all of his punches accept the one that caught her in the right eye. His hands tightened around her neck.
Adina ran to the laundry room where her mother kept a baseball bat on the top shelf. Her mother's cries were close to her ears. Adina returned to the miserable

atmosphere. She didn't quite understand the consequences of murder, she just wanted her father to stop beating on her mother as if she were a punching bag. "Daddy stop hitting her." Adina pleaded. Quinn shouts out at his heartbroken daughter.

"You shut up." He roared, kneeing Avah in the chest. She gasped for air barely able to see out of the black and blue eye Quinn had given her. Avah punched Quinn in the face making him even more mad.

"I hate you." Adina charged at her father banging him in the head with the bat until he fell unconscious. "Leave. Leave. Get out of here."

She's hysterically crying, screeching as she continues upside his head till she sees blood on her hands. Blacking out, the blood of her father stained on her palms, Adina took off running out of their shabby two story apartment into the brisk early morning foggy streets, wearing only a t-shirt and cheetah print socks. As she's racing down the haggard block, no real destination in mind, she floods right into the arms of Cashmere Jean. Blood on her shirt, pieces of her father's DNA beneath her nails, she's weeping a ton as she mangled backwards busting her ass onto the wasted concrete. Cashmere gawks at her. His first thought is damn *she's fine as hell.* The evidence on her hands sparked his curiousity, but he wasn't trying to catch heat fucking with her. He gapes at her before pulling the handle to go inside the store.

"I need help." Adina cringed, glaring at Cashmere's backside.

"Whoa, whoa, whoa lil mama," he says turning around. "You look like you got a lot going on shawty." Faltering to get involved, Cashmere stretched his hand out in doubt to cure her. "Don't touch me." Adina screamed. Afraid for any man to physically lay hands on her, she blurted,

"Don't come near me." The rocky cement brushing against her behind every time she'd scoot backwards. Cashmere emptied his pockets, holding his hands where Adina could see them. "Aye lil thang," he says, "I'm not gonna hurt--"*(Slow Motion)*

(Black Car Approaching)

The ending of his sentence was cut short by a bullet penetrating his torso. Going to pieces on his back, Cashmere deflated on the cracks of the concrete in front of the Windy City Mini Mart.
The kid Dorian, that he and Marco sprayed earlier for twenty dollars, came back on the warpath.
(Slow Motion)
   Life appeared as a gridlock, except the fireworks of the tires burning rubber on the ground.
Adina buried her face in her thighs blaring for a remedy. Time seemed to have gone still, giving up Casper, the friendly ghost. Everything came to a complete stop. Adina slithered over to Cashmere's almost late body on the rind of her knees. She compressed his shivering hand in hers.
   (Whispering)

   "I don't know who you are, but hold on okay," she says. "Breath with me." She nods at him. "Is there somebody you want me to call?"
   Her eyes twinkled under the streetlight. "Rafael." She screamed. Moments later, Rafael came darting out of the door. Blood covered the pavement.
   "Oh my God." He uttered, falling to his knees. "Who did this to you son?"

Cashmere's fading in and out, but somehow Adina's beauty struck him alive. He's staring at her doing the breathing exercises, a promising look of death in his eyes. Meanwhile, the bullet is on a roller coaster ride on his intestines, sweeping through his abdomen.

"Keep breathing with me." Adina hampered Cashmere gently in her arms. A junkie hiding out in a nearby alley called 911. Getting a glimpse of the face of the person lying on the ground, bleeding, the junkie came to realize it was Cashmere. "Shit." The fiend mumbled. "That's Mrs Elliana Jean's grandson."

(Ambulance Sirens) (Lights Flashing)

The crackhead sped off running down the decrepit sidewalk, staggering to Elliana Jeans house while Cashmere got put on a stretcher and taken to Methodist Hospital of Chicago.

Ext. 7:45AM Friday

Her first day out of the slammer, and boy was she clear on the deck to hit the scene and see where the money was at. First she had to pay a visit to her mother. Alexis sighed as she twisted the doorknob to her mother's house. Surprisingly it was locked. Times really have changed. Back in the day you could sleep with your windows open, blinds up and so forth. Tuh, not now you couldn't. You'd be risking getting robbed and killed. Alexis shouts, "Mama. I'm home. Open the door." To no avail there was no answer.

Alexis tested her surroundings. There wasn't a soul in sight whose phone she could use to call her mother. She left her one bag of unimportant shit on the porch taking a prowl through the old neighborhood. Then it dawned on her. In the safe days you could slip your spare key outside, underneath the flower pot or drop it in the mailbox. Hell, you could even give your neighbor an extra key. Alexis made a u-turn walking back to her mother's sanctuary. Say there was an extra key, she was going to use it, go straight upstairs to the bathroom and take a shower.   As she's searching for a way to get inside a voice not too familiar recognizes her. "Alexis Jean." Says the next door neighbor Mrs. Davina. "My God." Her voice cracked. "I haven't seen you in years. How are you doing child?"

   Off the rip Alexis's fond memory of the sweet lady came to her. She brought to mind that Sunday after church her mother, Mrs Davina and other neighbors were playing spades in the living room at her mother's house. All the kids had to go downstairs to the basement until the food was done cooking. One thing Alexis retained about her mother's long time friend was her son Quinn who she hadn't seen since going to prison. That was sixteen years ago.   "Don't just stand there like a statue." Mrs. Davina chuckles. "Give an old woman a hug."

   "Is my mother home?" Alexis asked, tying herself in the arms of an old friend. Mrs. Davina tightened her robe. She sat in her recliner chair taking her blue rollers out one by one sitting them on the table beside her. "I knocked a few times. Maybe she's up in her room sleeping."   "Child yo momma fled out of here earlier at sum four in the morning. She called me up saying she had to go to Methodist Hospital." Alexis nearly stopped breathing. She began panicking, asking a thousand questions.

   "Did she say why? Who drove her? Has she called you since she left this morning?"

   "Child you have been gone a long time."

   "Mrs Davina please just tell me what happened." Alexis whispers. "Is my mother okay?" The scowl on Mrs Davina's face wasn't very pleasant. She didn't feel it was her place to say anything. At the same time she broke the news to Alexis anyway.

"Child ya momma is fine."

"That's a relief." Alexis put the key in the door, hastening her way inward. A shower was calling her name from miles away. Mrs. Davina wasn't quite through talking though. The final part of her conversation hit Alexis like a bulldozer.

"It's your son you should be worrying about."

Alexis stopped. One foot in the door, one out. "What?" She says, "What's that supposed to mean?" She hissed, a whole mile of attitude in her voice. "I'll take care of my son ma'am. You worry about Quinn. I know his grown ass," Alexis said with, attitude, "Is still bad as hell." Her sarcastic response raised hairs on Mrs. Davina's arms. Mrs. Davina buzzed back with news she saw on television just a few hours before Alexis showed up.

"It was all on the news." Mrs Davina shared as she swayed back and forth in her chair.
"Cashmere Jean," she blinks, "16, shot in the abdomen earlier this morning."

Int. Inside Elliana Jeans House

Alexis misplaced every train of thought she had, the nauseating bubble in her stomach stirring round and round. She raced to her mother's bedroom finding it desolate. Clearly she'd been in bed hours ago. The blanket was rumpled up the pillows on the floor and the lamp left on. Alexis reached for the phone in nothing flat of a second to call her mother. "Pick up the phone momma." Alexis says, conversing with herself. After the fourth ring, she slams the phone down. Seconds pass and it rings. Unsure of what to do at first, Alexis didn't pick up on the first ring. By the third time she surrendered.

"Hello." She says, in a weary tone. Elliana burst out in a truck full of tears knowing it was her daughter's voice on the other end of the line.

"Momma are you okay?" Shortly tears of a little girl trapped inside of Alexis's body came running over her cheeks. "Momma where's--?" She lurched on her words carrying on what she had to say. "Where's my son?" She sputtered. Alexis exhaled a great deal of guilt as her eyes kept on filling up with water. "Where's my son?" She uttered in shame, clenching onto her dingy white t-shirt. Elliana sighed, disappointed in what the outcome would be once Cashmere tumbled out of retirement.

Chapter #2

Int. Methodist Hospital- Three Days Later 9pm Monday

Spouting his eyes free of shadiness, a wintertime chill kindled the hairs on Cashmere's bare-skinned arms. Right by his side, grasping his wound, Adina slept nuzzled up on his tiger chest snoring like a baby. Stirred up at the jangle of his heartbeat, the touch of his fingers on her lips, Adina cleared her vision to see Cashmere being sweet to her. "You're up." She says twisting the hairs on his chin. They were stuck in the groove, falling for each other. Mooning over her honey brown features wanting to lock lips with her, Cashmere held in his respect.

"Aye lil thang." He spoke, treasuring her blooming good looks. Also putting a smile on her face. She giggled.

"Hey you. How you feeling?"

"I feel like I got shot." Cashmere says, the dryness in his throat makes it hard for him to talk.   "I'm sorry love, I know it hurts." Adina kissed his stomach, the feathery activity of her lips supple on the frame of his torso. Spellbound by her eyes, Cashmere is deaden on her. "Does it hurt bad?" She enquired about caressing his chin.
   "Nah." His raspy reply, less painful.
"Not when you kiss it like that." (Silence)

7:31am Tuesday

Elliana Jean couldn't stay at the hospital due to her own health issues. Good thing she had her neighbor Mrs. Davina right next door in case of an emergency. The old time friends sat in Elliana Jean's living room. They drank black tea, ranting about their wacky teen years. As they chat, Alexis tramps through the door along with Quinn pinching her on the butt, presuming no one was home. Both their eyes are bloodshot red. The bag of weed they smoked seeped from their pores. Alexis sees her mother accompanied by Mrs. Davina.
   "Oh, hey momma." She says, acting normal. Her smile faded away. "Didn't know you were home."
   Mrs. Davina rolled her eyes to the back of her head, disgusted at her son. "I see you left Avah at home again to run the streets with another woman, getting high and shit."
   "Hold on." Alexis spat. "Avah?" She asked. "The Avah we grew up with?" She pressed for an answer. The only Avah, Alexis remembered, was dirty black ashy Avah from Kedzie Avenue with her fucked up box braids.
   Mrs. Davina shook her head. "Chile like I told you, you have been gone a long time." She sipped her tea. "Oh and he married the girl." She hissed, the hotness of her drink burning her top lip. "They have a fourteen year old

daughter." She laughs deviously. "Did you tell her that son?"

"Momma." Quinn got angry. "You need to be quiet."

"So where have you been Alexis?" Her mother inquisitively asked. "Ya ain't been to the hospital not once to check on that boy of yours."

"Momma I know." Irritated, not in the mood for her mother to judge her, she says, "I've been in the field, hustling to get back on my feet." She takes a Newport one hundred from the pocket of her baggy sweatpants. "Did you tell him I was home?"

"Whew gawd this girl," says Mrs. Davina referring to Alexis.

"Mind your business old lady, damn." Alexis strifed at her. "This conversation is between me and my mother." She said, bumping her gums. "Won't you C your way out the front door smelling like mothballs and shit"

"Oh hell no." Mrs Davina stomps her foot. "Hell no." She spit out. "Chile." She says. "Don't think because I'm old, I won't kick your high yellow ass." Davina rolls her neck around. "Elliana you better tell her how we used to get down." Alexis sparked her cancer stick.

"Whatever." She exhaled the smoke. Davina blatantly ignored Alexis. She glanced at the swollen knot on her son's head.

"What happened to your head Quinn?" She asked curiously.

"Your lunatic granddaughter beat me with a baseball bat."

"Hmph." She dryly sighed. "You must have deserved it." She hissed. "You've been putting your hands on Avah?" Mrs. Davina looks at Alexis. "Tuh! And honey if you think for one minute you're special," She chuckled, swallowing her tea. "It's only a matter of time before he starts whooping yo ass to."

"I don't have time for this." Alexis snarled. "Quinn let's go." She said, giving Mrs. Davina a sleazy eyed look. "Actually." She heads toward the bathroom. "Let me pee first."

Broke as hell, Alexis lied about needing to use the restroom. What she really did was went in her mother's stash taking five twenty dollar bills. Usually there was more money in the brown envelope. Alexis moved quietly to her son's room. She rummaged through his dresser drawers, the shelf of the closet. She found nothing. Desperate to find a dollar, Alexis searched one last place. She took one glance at Cashmere's bed. Mattresses were always good for hiding things. She slid the mattress toward her waist. There was a slit the size of a c-section alongside the mattress. Alexis dug her hand in it, pulling out the bag of cocaine Maggie had given to Cashmere. Her eyes glowed with dollar signs. She needed something to cover herself. She grabbed a hoodie from Cashmere's closet, hiding the bag inside of it.

Hip to Alexis's bad habits, Elliana stashed away the other half of her funds in Davina's attic. Alexis returned to the living room. Her mother stared at her. She wasn't nobody's fool. She knew good and well Alexis robbed her in plain sight.

"Whew gawd." Elliana sighed, weeping. "That girl is going to be the death of me."

Ext. Tuesday 12:30pm Kedzie Avenue

The weather had been bitterly cold all morning. Alexis ran the streets wearing nothing except a hoodie to keep her warm. Searching for a cocaine connection, Quinn up and says he's acquainted with a few people, connected to the Italians who would happily front her some work. Jumping head first into the Lion's den, Alexis asked him for a contact number. "You can't fuck around on them Alexis." Quinn tells her. "If they front you this work, you have to pay up. There's no running, hiding, none of that shit."

"Quinn." Alexis pats his arm. "I'm not new to these streets. The meatball eating motherfuckers doesn't scare me."

"Go ahead then." Quinn replies sarcastically. "Fuck with them if you want. You're gonna find ya moms dead in her basement with her fucking tongue cut out."

"Quinn if you got the number make the call."

Alexis spotted a homeless man standing in front of an abandoned building, drinking a forty. She slides up to him asking for a cigarette. Noticing they were also at a bus stop, Alexis went on to ask if he had any idea what time the next bus was coming. He unzips his oversized baggy coat pulling out a torn bus schedule. Alexis put her hand on his lower back. She eased her way to his back pocket where he kept his wallet. Taking her time, moving gradually, she retrieved the wallet passing it to Quinn as he walked by them.

"Yea. Um hmm." She said as the bum stuttered to tell her the times of transportation. "You hungry Mr?" She asked pretending to care or have feelings whether he ate today or not. She wound up leaving, not giving him a dime. "Be safe out here okay." Alexis met up with Quinn back at her mother's house.

"That was easy." Quinn shrugged laughing. "How much did we get?" Alexis burst out giggling.
"What'd you expect? He was drunk." She snickered. "And what do you mean, what do we get? This is my shit." She said. Her and Quinn went to her bedroom. Everything stayed the exact same from the time she went to prison in

2004. All her stuffed animals given to her from Cashmere's father when they were kids were lined up on her dresser. A bunch of tacs held pictures to the wall of her and Marco's mother Sadie. Quinn glared at the fun-filled photos.

"I know this chick."

"Yeh. That's my son's---" She started to say godmother, but Quinn rudely objected.

"Son? You have a child?" He was shocked by what she just said. "Is he here?" Bothered at Quinn wanting to be so damn inquisitive at the wrong time, she parted her lips simply answering his one of twenty five questions.

"No. He's not here."

"Where is he?"

"Oh my God Quinn." Alexis says, annoyed, slapping her knee as she's counting her pickpocket money. "He's not here. He's at the Methodist Hospital. He got shot. Now can you shut the fuck up and let me count my bread." Quinn nods his head. A cold stare came over his face. "Sixty, eighty, one hun--" Quinn raised his hand. He came down on Alexis like a helicopter out of the sky. His hand hit her across the face, permanently marking her cheek. Alexis gripped the dollar bills extra tight preventing him from getting any. She sprawled to her feet.

"Nigga who the hell do you think you're putting your hands on? I'm not your wife." She screamed, the loudness of her voice echoing in Quinn's ear. "I'm not Avah." She hollered, smacking him across the face with a stack of one dollar bills. "Nigga I will kill you."

Quinn pinned her to the wall, his forearm beneath her neck. "Bitch do something." He taunted her, gritting his teeth. "I'll break your motherfucking back." He shoves her to the bed. "Take your ma-fucking panties off. I want some pussy and I want it now." He demanded. Alexis removed her sweatpants along with her underwear. It'd been years since she had a good dick, so it kind of turned her on that Quinn was seconds away from dicking her down. He unlatched his leather belt, Alexis's eyes stuck to him as he beat his meat to get it stiff and going. He crawled between her thighs, nibbling on her neck. He let the tip of his shaft smack her pussy lips as he rinsed her mouth out using his tongue. Moaning, enjoying him, takes command of the twiddle in Alexis's vagina throbbed. She clawed at his back, wanting him to fuck her and quit the foreplay shit. "Quinn put it in daddy, please." She wheezed, invoking him to pine stroke her. "Stop teasing me." She breathed heavily as if it were her last breath. Quinn wiggled his manhood two inches to the right of her vagina and began giving her aspiring strokes. Peering for a breath to catch, eyes rolling back, Alexis squealed like a baby. She threw her legs over Quinn's shoulders. Thrusting into her wet ocean, he gave her abusive smooches on her lips. Wedging his butt cheeks together, he drove his hands and knees into the sheets clouting her g-spot. "Quinn pull out." Alexis moaned. Ignoring her request, he contracted her at the waist. "Quinn pull out." Alexis fought him. "You don't have a condom on." She hissed. He shut her up with a passionate kiss to her mouth.

"Damn." He groaned. "This pussy is super wet." His body stiffened. He thrust deeper into her, ejaculating inside of her. "Uurrggg." His body jerked. "Ummph, shit." Beads of sweat fell from his forehead on Alexis's breast. "Goddamn." He stayed inside of her, pumping to cum again. "I'm about to bust another nut." He said pressed against Alexis's g-spot. "Squirt for daddy." Alexis screamed out....

"Quinn, oh my God. Oh my fucking God. I'm gonna squirt." She sang. "I'm gonna--" Her heart rate sped up.

Her temperature skyrocketed through the roof. "Aahh. Aahhh... ummph baby." Alexis cried. Her pussy got wetter and wetter. She exploded, soaking the bed sheets. Holding Quinn close to her, not wanting to let him go, she kept her bare legs tied around his waist, grinding on his semi-hard stick until she came again and again.

Ext. Wednesday- 5am- Outside of Mattia's Club

"Renzo."
 Quinn yelled from the parking lot. "What up boi boi."
 Alexis got herself a good picture of Renzo. He was fine as hell, tall, brown skinned, and a print in his pants to go with his swag. Quinn turns to Alexis. "Let me do the talking, hear me? Don't open your mouth unless I say so." Renzo looked closer to see who was hollering his name at five in the morning. He loosened up on the trigger of his Smith and Wesson, realizing it was Quinn an old acquaintance of his. He locked the doors on his Navy blue Mustang. As he's walking toward Quinn, smoking a blunt, he gives Alexis a dirty stare. One thing about Renzo, he knew a bird bitch when he saw one. Alexis didn't quite present herself as such. She had on taupe thigh high boots, the skin tight, ripped blue jeans she wore hugged her thighs. Her breasts sat up perfectly in a fitted white belly shirt. Her faux fur coat kept away the cold that chased the hairs up her spine. A small amount of smoke gray eyeshadow brought a gloss out in her stolen brown eyes. Mac red lipstick accentuating her full lips. She eyed Renzo from head to toe. It seemed he had the wrong impression of her, so she went against Quinn's orders to speak and introduce herself.
 "Renzo." She said, "Hi." She reached to shake his hand. "I'm Alexis Jean." Renzo chuckles, inhaling a long drag of smoke. "You're Alexis Jean?" He asked, surprised. "I can

tell you right now baby girl, there ain't no good--" He puckered his luscious lips, "behind that name." He smirks. I bet money on it." He says, spitting on the ground. Alexis giggled.

  Quinn wanted to holler at Renzo privately since Alexis decided to make a grand goddamn introduction. He nods at Renzo to take a walk with him. As they walked side by side, Quinn inhaled the weed into his lungs. He whispered out of range, asking Renzo if he still had any connections to the Italian boss Alessandro. Renzo didn't deny it, he also didn't admit if he was or not.

  "My girl wants some work." Quinn says looking back at Alexis.

  "Ummm." Renzo says unsure. "I don't know about that one bruh.

  Alexis approached Quinn and Renzo.

  "Are we in or not?"

Renzo definitely wasn't feeling Alexis. Her ghetto vibes gave him an uncomfortable tickle in his stomach. "Slow down shorty." He tells her. "It's not that simple." He meets her face to face. His lips an inch away from hers. "It's levels to this shit mami."

  "Tuh!" Alexis grits her teeth. "I'll see you later Quinn. I'm going home. Give me the keys to the car."

  "Nah. You can wait." He scratched the corner of his lip using the tip of his thumb.

  "Quinn." Alexis shouts. "I'm going home. Give me the fucking keys."

Renzo wasn't with the messy shit at all. He removed himself. Quinn and Alexis stood there arguing. Quinn was mad as hell. Here he was trying to put Alexis on and she wanted to cause a scene and act like a damn fool. As soon as Renzo disappeared into Alessandro's club, he went upside Alexis's head, knocking her on her ass. He grabbed her at the ankles, sledding her across the concrete dents in the parking lot on her back. She's screaming, kicking at him with her boots.

"Fuck you Quinn." She blabbed her gums. "Fuck you, broke ass, can't make shit happen ass nigga." Quinn slammed her against the passenger door of his car.

"Get the fuck in the car, stupid ass hoe."

"I gotcha hoe nigga." Alexis leaned forward, spitting in Quinn's face. "I told you before." She says struggling to get her breathing under control, cleaning the dirt off of her coat. "I'm not Avah." She retrieves a pistol from her handbag. Quinn's eyes popped out of his head. He put his hands up, spit dripping down his face.

"I told you let me talk, but no, you had to be fucking hard headed talking about "*Heeyyy, I'm*

Alexis Jean, tryna be all cute and shit."

"I did sixteen years at Pontiac prison for being an accomplice to a murder." Alexis began to cry. "Don't make me kill you Quinn, or else Avah will have to strip and suck dick to pay for your funeral with her broke ass." Her eyes were full of the truth of what she was capable of doing. She cocked the gun back. "Now give me the keys." She demanded. Quinn wiped the saliva from his cheek putting the keys in Alexis's hand.

Ext. Thursday- Cashmere Comes Home

Adina thanked Mrs Davina for giving her and Cashmere a ride home. More able bodied than his grandmother, Davina offered to carry his bag in the house while Adina assisted him in walking up the steps. Having a hard time focusing on where he was at, Cashmere observed his surroundings.

The morphine had him drowsy and out of it. The address to his house didn't seem right. He's staring at the numbers, in his eyes they're blurry, seeming so far away. Shivering to get out the rain, Cashmere groaned. He walked as slowly as someone's ninety year old grandmother. Adina took her time with him, seeing to it that he didn't trip over his own feet.

"Your grandmother must be cooking. I smell biscuits." Mrs Davina said smiling. She knocked on the screen door.

"We're here." She says holding the door open for Adina and Cashmere. Although he moved at a snail-like pace, she patiently waited for them to get up the steps. Once they were all in from January's winter weather, Davina put her purse down, closing the door behind her. It wasn't her dear friend in the kitchen cooking up a storm.

Int. Living room- 9am

"Quinn baby your food--" Alexis comes into the living room. The first person she saw was her son. "Oh my--" She burst out in tears. Quinn's plate shattered to the floor. "Oh my God, son." She cried. "How did you--" She hugged him. "Are you alright? Are you okay?" Cashmere reacted to his mother like the stranger she was. He avoided her affection, wondering who in the fuck was this grown ass man on his grandmother's couch. Adina cringed at the sight of her father. The night of him abusing her mother played back in her head.

"Where's your bedroom?" She asked Cashmere. Her stomach got queasy as if she were going to throw up. Before her father knew she was under the same roof as him, she vanished to Cashmere's resting place. Cashmere's anger came out in the open.

"Why you got this bum ass ninja on my grandmother's couch, snoring and shit?" "I'm still your mother Cashmere." Alexis spat. "Watch your mouth."

Elliana Jean woke up out of her sleep to a bunch of screaming and cursing. She wobbles to the living room on her walker in a nightgown.

"He's my fucking man." Alexis yells. "That's why he's here."

"Chile," says Davina. "The man is married for God's sake. You're just a wet ass, and a slap in the face."

"What is going on here?" Elliana wanted to know. Cashmere's eyes lit up seeing his grandmother. His entire life revolved around her. She was the one who kept him together when his mother went to prison. If it wasn't for her, he'd be in foster care.

"NaNa you okay?" He kissed her cheek. "Don't worry. Me and Marco gone take care of this nigga."

"Aht." She says, "Now you know I raised you better than that Cashmere Jean."

"Yes ma'am." Cashmere replied. The relationship between him and his grandmother raised hairs on Alexis's spine. She hooped, hollering about Cashmere disrespecting her as if she weren't his mother. But how could he respect someone who wasn't there for him? Alexis was a total stranger, someone he didn't know.

"Oh I see." She blabbed. "You think ya granny is a goddamn saint huh." She laughed. "I bet she didn't tell you that she used to be a drug dealer." Alexis folds her arms. "Tell him momma. Tell him how you and daddy bought yachts, luxurious cars, houses, all with drug money."

"Alexis you close your mouth right now or else." Elliana coughed. "That was a long time ago."

She murmured. "Your son doesn't even know who you are."

"NaNa." Cashmere questioned her for the first time ever. "Is it true?" His voice cracked. "You and granddad were drug dealers?"

"Oh they were big time." Alexis made it known.

"Get out of my house." Elliana wept. "Take your married man and getcho ass out." She uttered. "Tuh." Alexis sucked her teeth. "You only have to tell me once." She said slamming the door leaving.

Chapter #3

Int. 1pm Thursday

Four hours later, after all the bickering that took place earlier that morning, Adina opened her eyes to Cashmere going through some of his grandparents' old photos. One person he recognized in particular was his grandmother. In total disbelief of what he saw in the pictures, he grew angry. All the times Elliana worried about him and Marco getting killed, yet there she was in photos with his grandfather Jesse. There were drugs, money, guns, and other women. In a second memory, there was Elliana laughing with a beautiful, thick light skinned girl who looked to be about seventeen, eighteen years old. They had guns in their laps, smoking weed. Their smiles were so radiant. One more familiar face struck Cashmere's nerves. His grandfather Jesse. He was captured sitting at a round table, bagging up cocaine, Ayinda to the right of him holding up his 22 and middle finger.

"Who are those people?" Asked Adina towering over Cashmere's shoulder. Cashmere clenched his jaws together. His eyes got wide.

"Would you believe me if I said they're my grandparents?" He turns toward her answering her question, his face as red as a cherry. "My fucking grandparents." He sighed. "All this time fronting like a saint and shit."

"I have a confession." Adina says. "The guy that was on your grandmother's couch is my father."

"What the f---" Cashmere went ballistic. "So, what." He says, "We're brother and sister or some shit."

"No." Adina screeched, crying, tears rolling down her cheeks. "The night you shot, I ran away from home. My dad is abusive." Adina proceeded to render herself. "I don't wanna go home." She sobbed. "I can't go home as long as he's there."

Cashmere pretty much had an advanced inkling of why Adina had blood all over her the night they met. Terror-stricken as if she committed the worst crime ever, Cashmere recalled the blood stains on her shirt and hands. She was terrified of him touching her. Keeping watch on her, Cashmere felt down in the dumps for her. After all, his mother missed out on him growing up, becoming a man. He didn't have a father around, coaching him on how to be a man. It was his grandmother who advised him while his absent, forbearing parents weren't there.

"Forget it." Adina wept, walking toward the door to freedom in the same t-shirt, socks she had on three days ago. "I don't need you. It's not like we really know each other anyway, right?" She shrugged her shoulders. The second she grabbed hold of the doorknob, Cashmere stopped her, staggering up behind her. He held her hand, releasing it from the knob.

"Stay." He pleaded.

Froze in the moment, Cashmere's pure aura comforted Adina in ways she's never felt, not even from her father or mother. Neither one of them had bathed in almost four days, a tart taste on their tongues. Adina's body cried for soap and water. The stench of not washing began to seep out of her. Meanwhile Cashmere needed deodorant like yesterday. Sleep was plastered on his face, crust in his eyes. Adina glared at him. Seeing beyond his physical appearance, mentally he attracted her. He had that sexy, innocent, bad boy vibe going on.

"You can take a shower if you want." Cashmere said, giving her a towel and washcloth. "Imma go check on my g-ma."

Limping to the door, Marco came barging in. "Who the fuck shot you bro?" He cocks his gun back. "We can go blast them niggas right fucking now bruh." In every sense of the word loose cannon is how you could describe Marco. True to the thug life, he was down for anything. He came in dressed in an all black Champion sweatsuit. His twists hanging to his shoulders.
Tattoos engraved on the skin of his hands. "So wassup?" He folds his arms.

"What we doing?" The expression on Marco's face is easy to read. He was ready to murder someone. He stood there bowlegged, contemplating putting a bullet in somebody's head. "Pop a perc or whatever the fuck you on and let's go get these niggas bruh." Adina sat in silence the whole time until Marco mentioned going on a killing spree. She gazed at Cashmere picturing him getting shot. Had she not been there that night, chances are, he would have died.

"Go take a shower." He tells her. "Let me rap with my brother alone."

On the way out the door, Marco looked Adina up and down. She had slim thick, juicy thighs, baby watermelon sized breasts and pretty toes. That put the cherry on the cake. Neither Cashmere or Marco could stand a female with ugly feet. Marco laid the bullets to his Smith and Wesson gun on Cashmere's bed. They were about to load the clip when Alexis walked herself in, uninvited with her stank ass attitude. Marco was only three when she went to prison, but his mother spoke of her often. He'd seen wild pictures of Alexis and his mother when he was younger, so he recognized her face. He especially noticed her big lips. Cashmere on the other hand wasn't the least bit thrilled to be in her presence.

"Do you knock?" He asked in a nonchalant way. Alexis did what any black mom would do when being questioned by a kid. She crossed her arms over her chest.

"Do I knock! What the fuck you mean do I knock? I may have just gotten out of jail and we ain't all that cool, but watch ya mouth, I'm still ya mother!" Alexis scolded her only child. "You have no reason to speak to me like that. I went to jail tryna put food in ya mouth and clothes on my back. Ya daddy ain't do shit and by the way this is my mama's house. Ya lil ass don't pay no damn bills to question if I knock or not. I'll knock ya ass clean out." She spat at him. "How bout that."

Cashmere mustered up every bit of breath in his body. It took an insane amount of pain for him to raise his tone at his mother.

"I don't pay bills, but I cook." He yelled. "I do laundry." He beat on his chest. "Where were you when NaNa needed you?"

The animosity in the room grew bigger than all of them. Cashmere's eyes bulged out of his sockets. His veins pumped adrenaline. Alexis and he exchanged gruesome stares at each other.

"Why are you even here?" He muttered. "Ya own mother told you to leave. Why are you back?" He quizzed.

Alexis raised her hand as if she were going to sting Cashmere. Marco hated to see them going at it. He got in the middle of them.

"Come on now godmom." He says, playing the mediator for once in his chaotic life. "Y'all both need to chill the fuck out."

"Man whatever." Cashmere rose to his feet, pushing past his mother." It killed him to stand up. He just couldn't force himself to be in the same room with the woman who left him to be raised by his grandmother. Although living with his grandma wasn't all that horrible. As he was leaving, Alexis cursed him out.

"I don't need to do shit." She hollered. "His lil ass disrespected me and you better not start with me or you're next. Yall lil mfs gone learn today, I'm not the one but since I am grown I'll holla at y'all lil asses later. I got shit to do." Alexis almost forgot, she hadn't smoked any weed yet. "Oh and before I go." She said. "I'm sure y'all smoke. Where is the weed?" She stared at Marco. "I need some good shit. It's been a minute since we had some good shit upstate."

Adina just happened to come into the room. She stopped right where she was, embarrassed to be half naked in front of people she didn't know. Alexis rolled her eyes.

"See you got ya lil hoes all up in here." Marco didn't want the situation to escalate more than it already had. He had a dime bag in his pocket, a Dutch and a yellow Bic lighter.

"Let's go roll this weed up." He insisted. Him and Akexis walked down the hall to her bedroom. They cracked the window, smoking a blunt all to themselves while catching up on what prison life was like.

CONTIN...

Left alone to get formally acquainted with one another, Cashmere and Adina kicked it in his room for a while. There were a lot of questions Adina wanted to ask. At the same time, she didn't want to come on too strong. One thing for sure, that shower brought her back to life again. She was beginning to smell like rotten eggs. She rolled her dirty clothes up in a ball. "Where do I put these?" She says, holding eye contact with Cashmere, who's observing her chocolate brown complexion. A sight for sore eyes, Adina saw a white tee folded on the bed with a pair of red nautica boxers and black ankle socks.

"Can I put this on?" Her towel fell to the floor, revealing her mini pancake shaped nipples. Stuck on Adina's sculptural physique, Cashmere undressed himself as best he could. While attempting to lean over and take his socks off, his abdomen began to burn. He was all tore up inside, suffering through his tender wound. "Aarrgghh." He groused in distress, battering his fist into the floor. "Gimme a perc." He appealed to Adina. Claiming his summon, Adina got her hands on the orange medicine bottle, popping the cap off. In fine print the instructions clearly said take one pill every six hours. Adina shook the vial until a pill slid in the palm of her hand. "I need two." Cashmere griped at her. Adina wasn't at all steadfast on him taking more than one, eight hundred milligram pellets, however she obliged to his vexatious pleas.

Int. Day #2- 5pm Friday

(Slow Motion) (Tires Screeching)

*Adina's crawling on the ground as if she were a four legged animal.***(BANG)***Cashmere's gasping for air, up in arms, sparring to stay alive. "I don't know who you are, but breathe with me okay. Breathe with me."*

(Adina's voice fades)

   Irresistible even in his sleep, Adina eased her fingers over Cashmere's bandage. She planted kisses on his chest, her lips as soft as rose petals. Cashmere freed his eyes of the nightmare he was having, wishing he was dreaming, he woke up dizzy, half unconscious, but never lost memory of the texture of Adina's delicate, ginger skin tone. He stroked her cheek, glad to have woken up beside her. Weak for him, she rubbed his belly wanting to note just how defective his gash really was.

   "I wanna see your scar." She murmurs, gently peeling the tape off of his stomach.

Cashmere laid still, glaring at Adina as she took her time revealing his bruise. To her wonder his flaw made her smile. She melted her hands on him, leaning forward kissing the medium sized scab. The funny feeling of them being bound together brought in a sweat. Adina flew high around Cashmere. She was content laying up under his funky ass even though he still hadn't showered yet. Making small talk, keeping the handwriting on the wall, Adina sounded out a few inquiries of her own.

   "Do you know your spirit animal?" She enquired. Her voice sugared like candy.   "Talking about spirit animals." Cashmere managed to snicker. "We don't even know each other's name shawty." Adina sniggled, the probe of her hand meeting his. She frisked his torso, bringing him peace of mind more so than the Percocet pills that were prescribed to him for his torment. Better apprised of each,

Cashmere retained having to do his grandmother's laundry.

"Damn." He uttered beneath his breath.

"What? What's the matter?" Adina sat up.

"Oh, nah. Nothing." Cashmere echoed. "It's Friday." He squelched. His stomach ached just a bit. "I gotta do my grandma's laundry."

"I can give you a hand if you want," says Adina standing up to get dressed. "Are you ready to go now?" She buzzed.

(Knock Knock) Cashmere's grandmother comes into his room

"Oh," she says, "Well who is this?" She inquired, her voice gruff and dry. "Cashmere you know

I don't play about these fast behind girls in my house."

Using the manners learned to her by her mother, Adina introduced herself. Her well-behaved personality was a relief to Cashmere's grandmother. She sized Adina up, head to toe. A few moments of silence, Cashmere made it known; that Adina was offering to help him wash her clothes. That being the least of Elliana's concern, she came to talk to Cashmere about the pictures he discovered. A life she lived in her past obviously caught up to her. She imagined how Cashmere felt finding out that she and his grandfather were two of Southside Chicago's biggest heroin dealers. In the end none of it was worth it. Everything they bought with drug money, the houses, condos, cars, was no longer in their possession. All the things they worked for legally they happily owned, for example the house they've been living in since Cashmere was born.

"Sweet pea." She says. "I know what you're thinking. And I promise you," she convinced him, coughing up words of self-accusation. "I gave that life up long ago." She said using her walker to escort her to the bed.

"I knew the moment you came into this world, the day your mother went to pris--" Brazenly, Cashmere interrupted his grandmother while talking, something he's never done before. Usually they communicated well. This time he felt an outburst of resentment toward her. These pictures weren't lying. That was for damn sure.

"What did she go to prison for? Selling drugs." Cashmere said, with a smart mouth, shrugging his shoulders. "The Apple doesn't fall far from the tree, does it." He emphasized. The draft of Elliana's hand met Cashmere's face, leaving a long-lasting red print on his cheek. Adina could do nothing except console him. "The fuck off me yo."

He retorted, pulling away from her. "Just listen to her babe." Adina pleaded, squeezing his hand.

Marco's crazy ass burst in mid conversation, pistol on his hip a blunt behind his ear. "Yo you ready to run up on these bitch ass niggas?" His throat went dry. He didn't expect to see Elliana standing there. "Hey NaNa." He toned down the hype putting a set of kisses on her cheek . "You need anything? You good?" He transposed from gangster to an upright, pristine teenager right before Elliana's eyes.

"You ain't gotta front no more bruh." Cashmere googled his grandmother in the eyes. "She is a drug dealer. She's the biggest hustler in Chicago. Tell him NaNa." Cashmere got the proof off the dresser. "You don't believe me? Here." He tossed photos at Marco.

"Babe stop." Adina began to argue with him.

Marco glared at the drawing of Elliana and Jesse. "Told you I wasn't lying." Cashmere said. All Marco could say was "*damn.*"   Afterall Elliana couldn't escape her past.

She thought she'd buried that part of her life away for good.

Day #3 9:30pm Saturday

Int. Bedroom- Night

(Cashmere's

Dreaming) (Gunshots)

(Adina's Voice)

Breath, breath!! Aye lil

thang!!

(Cashmere wakes up in a sweat)

Waking up in the faint of his room, lying in his full size bed, numb as if he'd been shot again, a tear slid down Cashmere's cheek. He crouched, seeking his body for bullet holes finding none other than the wound covered in white bandages. Saturated in what he hallucinated to be a pool of blood, he perspired. The hunger pains living in his stomach made him want to get up on his feet and raid the kitchen. Three days without an appetite, he was now craving something big to feast on. Striving for energy, he tried his hardest to push the massive comforter off of him without breaking his back. Easing his way out from under Adina's arm, careful not to wake her, he slid out of bed. "Umph." He grumbled, barely standing up straight. Panting as he put one foot in front of the other, he grew flaccid. In the shadows of his bedroom, he settled in the same spot where he stood for two minutes too long.

"Adina." He gasped.

His stomach punished him to have a seat and repose himself. Adina had rolled over to a voided spot and the presence of Cashmere was not there. She scrambled out of bed.

"Babe." She said, turning on the lamp the light blinding her. "You okay? What are you doing?" "I'm hungry as hell." He snarled. "And my damn stomach hurts." A knockout pill would only put Cashmere back to sleep.

He had enough as it is. The illusion of closing his eyes haunted him. He wanted to be on guard for as long as he could be. Rather than walking out to the kitchen, he glided, Adina right there with him in case he needed her. Walking arm in arm, the closer they got to the cook's room, the harmony of the blues, wordlessly vibrated. In the kitchenette area at the modern, powered blue wooden table, Elliana gave her feet a rest as she sipped a hot cup of black tea, tears streaming down her pretty brown face. Cashmere gazed at his grandmother. He wanted to turn right back around and go to his room, but he didn't. "Tsk. Psshh." He sucked his teeth, reaching in the cabinet for a plate.

"I fell in love with your grandfather when I was thirteen years old." Elliana snivels. "We were young," she says, evoking fond memories of herself and him. "We turned eighteen and got married." She chuckled, a sorrowful look on her face. "He had it all." She related to Cashmere, Adina listening to every word. "He gave me the world." As she's telling her story, she slips back in time. The foreign cars she drove, the money she and Jesse made. They were living the life. "He gave me the world using drug money." Her eyes water. "We went on trips, shopping sprees in Hawaii. You name it, we had it."

"NaNa I just came here for something to eat aiight." Elliana's emotions flared up. She burst out crying.

"I could never love a man the way I loved your grandfather. He was my life. Then--" Her brows grew close together. She clutched onto the handle of her walker, straining her thin fingers. "I found out he cheated on me--" The gun shots vivid in her thoughts as the day it happened. "With one of my closest friends, Essence."

Elliana's expression went to rest. "That hoe betrayed me. She violated the girl code." The name Essence changed Cashmere's attitude toward his grandmother. Hearing her say it, he knew she was talking about the gorgeous girl in the picture with her. Curious as to what happened to her, he asked.

"Is she still around?"

Adina had already figured out the answer to Cashmere's poll. His grandmother murdered Essence in cold blood. Whether Elliana affirmed it verbally or not, Adina's gut said she did.

Chapter #4

Int. Sunday- 8am

This Sunday morning Cashmere chose to stay home from church. Knowing his grandmother would bark up the tree and argue him to death about it, he locked his bedroom door, avoiding having to hear her mouth about it. As he predicted, she knocked on his door, unable to get in.

He spoke loud and clear, notifying her that he wasn't going. "Cashmere Jean." She said.
"Unlock this door right now." Wobbling to his feet, he did as his grandmother told him. Cashmere rolled his eyes. He could never fully comprehend why folks got all dressed up, wearing outrageous, expensive clothes, huge hats and alligator shoes to worship something or someone they've never physically seen before. He beamed at his grandmother in her oversized purple hat, two piece purple jacket and skirt, black tights and her flat slip on shoes. She used her cane to push open the door. She stood there silent as Cashmere did the same thing.

"I'm not going NaNa." He said.

"Tuh." She scowled. "Like hell you're not." Her face is serious and frightening. "Boy." She said,
"You better getcho' ass dressed. We're going to the house of the Lord."

Hour and A Half Later

The Pastor of New Beginnings Church of Chicago, Yindu Moco shouted in his deep African voice. "It's offering time." Every member in the congregation clapped, hollering Amen, praising the Lord. To some people, gospel music soothed the soul. The drummer screamed, hallelujah the pianist whimpering as he played the keys to No Weapon Formed Against Me Shall Prosper. When the usher came to Cashmere with a gold plate in her hand, he shook his head no. The look of disgust showed on her face. Elliana gapes at Cashmere with sweetish, cold eyes. "You better act like you know." She nods toward the plate of giving. The unanswered questions in Cashmere's head, seized him to pay any cash he had in his possession, forward to a God he'd never seen. He examined the members paying ten to one hundred dollars. Even his grandmother dropped a fifty dollar bill into the basket. When the usher turned her head, Cashmere retrieved the money from the pot putting it in his pocket.

"Baaabe." Adina gasped, silently laughing until her cheeks hurt."

"Nah." Cashmere whispers. "Fuck that." He said. "Pastor thinks he's getting rich off my grandma." He grits his teeth. "Ain't happenin bruh." He shrugs. "So." He glares at Adina. His Nike sweatpants fit her body like a wrapper to a piece of candy. "Praise the Lord and pass the pussy." He says, seductively eyeing her down as he put his hand down the crack of her ass.(*Adina laughing*)

"You're out of control sir."

4pm

Elliana was beginning to wonder how much longer Adina would be staying at her house. However, she didn't press the young beauty to go home where she belonged. Adina was sweet, helpful, willing to give her a hand in preparing Sunday dinner. "I can season the greens," she says, washing her hands at the sink. "I have nothing to do." She shrugs. "Since your grandson is sleeping." She sighed, smiling. "Again." She laughs. Hesitant at first, Elliana took in consideration Adina's manners and her cleanliness before touching the food. As they get the ingredients together there's complete secrecy between them. At the same time the dead air didn't bar Adina's composure. This was the utmost tranquility she's had in a long time.
(Doorbell rings)
(Indistinguishable chatter)

Adina cut the greens with style. She rolled it as if it were a blunt, then sliced it, the ridges of the knife separating the leafs from the stem. Glaring at her from behind, you'd imagine her as one of the elders at a church function. (Front door closes) Elliana liked for her kitchen to be organized when cooking. Adina didn't want to assume anything that Elliana may not want done in her home. The stockpot on the stove most likely was on low for the greens. Adina cleaned every leaf, rinsing it in warm water when Elliana rejoined her. Adina shut the water off. She put her hand on Elliana's lower back making sure she didn't fall.

"Is that kettle you have on the stove for the greens?" She inquired. Elliana could hardly blot out how impressed she was with the way Adina spoke.

"Kettle."

A smile spread across her fine wrinkled cheeks.

"You are an old soul."

In sync they cackled, the aroma of soul food up in the air as they commenced in good conversation. Adina took a moment to go check on Cashmere. He still hadn't showered. She laid the knife on the cutting board, excusing herself. "I'm gonna go see if your grandchild is awake." Cashmere was actually just getting out of bed when Adina walked in his room. He mantled at the sight of her adorable face.

"Still here I see."

Horsing around, Adina laughs. "I can leave if you want." She leans on the wall, crossing her arms.

"Nah."

Cashmere slithered over to her.

"I want you here." He lifts her chin, gawking her in the eyes. He put his arms around the small of her back

clinching onto her. No logic whatsoever, Adina cherished his fine, funky ass. His endearing smile obliging her.
(Knock At The Door) (Indistinct Chatter)

Avah showed up unannounced on Elliana's doorstep to pick her daughter up. Her pinch brown face is as tight as a button. She hadn't seen or heard from Adina since the fight with her father. Elliana glared at the scars on Avah's bronze cheeks. Maybe it was best that Adina didn't go home all week. Her mother wore the look of stress as if it were a Fashion Nova outfit. She shivered in a knitted sweater, and house slippers. Her hair in two pigtails, Chinese bangs cut to her eyebrows. As fine as she was, sleep definitely had nothing on the bags beneath her swollen eyes. Avah paced the porch, marking time until Adina came to the door. When Avah was finally able to look at her daughter, she cursed her out something unpleasant. The words parting her lips offensive and vile.
"Lets fucking go." She said, "Right now Adina."
"Ma I can't, you know why." Adina gapes backward at Cashmere. "He needs me." She looks her mother in the eye. "And he beats you ma." She uttered. The tears in her eyes are big as gum balls. "I'm tired of seeing him beat on you." She whimpered.

Because Adina had been sweet and respectful in the presence of her home, Elliana found no legit reason for her not to be there other than her mother saying she wanted her to leave. Avah, furious as hell kept shit going, hurting Adina's feelings. Elliana suggested for Avah to come inside. The wind had blown through the door giving the living room a cold chill. Avah kindly rejected Elliana's invite then decided to step in. She wanted to go home, but wasn't doing so without taking Adina with her.

"Now Adina."

She pestered her daughter. Adina sighed, the tears flowing rapidly down her cheeks. Cashmere's stomach fell to the floor as he minded Adina being snatched from him. Avah cracked a smile.

"Your father is home waiting for us to get back. He said, he's sorry about that night. He promised to never ever hit me again." Avah knew in her heart that wasn't true. Gifts may have worked for her. Adina could care less.

"He told me to give this to you."

Avah pulls a black, rectangular box from behind her back. She's forcing herself to be gracious.

"Open it." She urged.

"Mom." Adina says, dying on her words. Her throat congested. Her eyes bloodshot red.

"I love you." She gags. "I can't go home to that bastard."

She obstructs, erasing the water stains from her eyes with the palm of her hand. Cashmere gripped Adina in his arms. Her five foot figure against the trunk of his chest.

"I'm never gonna let anyone hurt you." He tells her, kissing her on the forehead. "And I put that on everything."

Elliana walked Avah to the front door on her assistance walker.

"As a mother." She began to say, sharing Avah's sorrows. "I know why you're here." She coughs. "But that child doesn't want to go home."

"And with all do respect." Avah snapped back. "I didn't ask her if she wanted to." Elliana sighed.

"Adina let's make it. It's cold. Your father is home waiting. Come on now." She says, stinging her daughter with her mean disagreement.

Ext. One Month Later- 12/31- Tuesday

Cashmere bolted out in the streets more than ever before, messing around on the ave knowing damn well that's stomping grounds for one-way tickets toward antisocial behavior. Only his grandmother's prayers were going to save him. Infringement was bound to catch up to him. Either that or he was going to end up dead or in jail. Him and Marco ransacked crooked cops. They made forbidden deals with cops like Finley and Greer, promising not to report them for doing shady business. Cops like Finley were bribing them, paying each of them a grand to keep their dirty activities underground. Living on the Southside of Chicago meant more carnage, more black mother's burying their sons and husband's. It definitely alluded to the police getting their cut in massacre cases, confiscating thousands of dollars in drug money. Rather than locking up the documentation, Finley, Greer and Williams would pocket the money. Honestly they were just sick and tired of black on black crime.

Ext: Garfield Park- Later That Day

(Wind Blowing)

Cashmere hit the winter streets dressed in a black and white Nike sweatsuit. He wore the new black and white LeBron sneakers and a red skully on his head to protect his ears from the harsh wind. Tucked on the inside pocket of his North Face coat was Pee Wee's 24k gold necklace and a couple hundred dollar bills. As Cashmere is heading toward Kedzie Ave, his mind falls back to that horrid day of Pee Wee's mother screaming her brains out. He steps off of the sidewalk standing exactly where Pee Wee died. Traces of his blood engraved in the crevice of the street.

(Flashback)

"God don't take my baby. God don't take my baby."

(Hysterical Screaming)

Pieces of yellow tape were lying on the ground. Cashmere knelt down staring at the broken letters.(Honk Honk) Cashmere stood to his feet leaving the half cut tape behind him as the car passed him by yelling, "Stay the fuck outta the street." Ahead of him sitting on the bench, Marco exhaled a balloon of smoke. He didn't bob up to be in the best mood. It was obvious something was paddling his mind. His actions expressed melancholy on his face and in his voice.

Cashmere hopped up on the tabletop, his legs spread apart, his elbows resting on his knees.

Marco barely said a word. He puffed on his weed letting the grey smoke out into the air.

"Yo, are you cool?" Cashmere asked, clapping his hands together. "Wassup?"

Cashmere's discussion of the matter went in Marco's ear and out the other until he opened up with the news of heartache. Moments ago he found out his mother Sa'lann was never coming home. The judge hit her with a life sentence without possibility of parole whatsoever. The life changing tragedy had Marco feeling as if he couldn't live another day. The void in his heart was so damn bad, he couldn't function on anything except robbing the next ma fucker that even looked at him the wrong way. Taking a long pull on his blunt, he asked Cashmere a selfsame question. Because at the end of the day, you only get one mother. And Marco loved his mother despite her flaws.

"You love ya moms bro?" Was Marco's question. His eyes are red, bulging outward. Quite honestly, Cashmere hadn't thought of how he felt about his mother. She missed such a huge part of his life, to him it was what it was. Either she was going to be a mother or she wasn't. Cashmere wasn't going to beg her to play the role.

He shrugged his shoulders. "I mean, how can I love someone--" He laughs, a sad giggle in his voice, "Who was never there for me?" He says, rubbing his hands against each other. Marco sighed as he faced his blunt to himself getting high as a kite.

"What's going on bruh?" Cashmere's voice cracked. Marco's eyes welled up with tears. His ears are as red as a cherry tree. "My mom's got life." He said rocketing to his feet, pacing the soil of the stone cold ground. "I feel fucking hopeless bruh." The weed was the only thing sustaining him, but the pain seemed to creep to the surface. "She might as well be fucking dead bruh." He looks over at Cashmere, devastation in his eyes.

"Damn bruh." Cashmere's head fell low. He pulled Marco into a man hug, slapping him on the back. "We're gonna survive together, aight."

Cashmere hadn't seen Adina in a month. He missed her smile and the sensitivity in her voice. He and Marco knew Kedzie Avenue well. Adina's house wouldn't be hard to find. Cashmere flipped his hood over his head.

"Bruh take this walk with me."

Marco hits the last of his blunt leaving the roach on the ground.
(Indistinct chatter)
(Shots Fired)

(Shots Fired)
(Shots Fired)
  "Oh shit." Marco said.
  "Goddamn." Cashmere stopped.

His stomach is turning in circles. He began feeling as though he was immersed in a bang up, like someone was poking him with a hot needle. Everything in the vicinity of his vision had the features of blood on it, the nose of his own death right before his eyes. Stuck in an insensible trance as to how it pinched his brain being shot, Cashmere's body went numb. Marco's hollering. "Nigga lets go clean this nigga pockets before the cops get here." Bouncing back to the name of the game, they ran over to the dead corpse. They emptied dudes pockets taking everything he had on him, winning three g's, all hundreds and twenty dollar bills. Marco arched the body over checking for drugs. In the pants pocket of the guy was bags of cocaine. He tossed it to Cashmere.   "Take this." He said.
   Cashmere searched the man for weapons, but instead erected a silver blade. His face turned sour. "Awl hell no bruh. The fuck is this."
(Cop Sirens)
(Lights Flashing)
(Tires Screeching)
   Before Cashmere and Marco knew it, Finley was on their asses along with three other bitch ass officers, Williams and Paige Greer. One of them is a rookie, Don Baines. Finley withdrew his glock .22 insisting that Cashmere and Marco give him the evidence they'd just poached off of a dead man's body. Already in a bad head space, Marco flipped the table on all four suckas.   "We not giving y'all bitch ass niggas shit." He said, sucking on his bottom lip.

Baines, skittish as can be at first put his emotions to the side. He raised his Smith and Wesson. "Give us the fucking money." He yelped.

"We not giving y'all crooked ma fuckas nuffin bruh." Cashmere howled. Baines shot Finley in an apprehensive flame. He stared back and forth at his colleagues.

"Williams, Williams." Baines screeched. "What the fuck is he talking about?" He bellowed. Finley accorded Williams to lay hands on Cashmere. "You wanna play tough?" He laughs deviously, grappling Cashmere in his white Nike sweatsuit. "I got your tough mother fucker."
Cashmere scuffled against Williams, throwing a jab to his jaw. Real quick, he retrieved his pistol.

"What we doing?"

Marco couldn't believe what was happening. Never ever had he clocked this kind of behavior coming from Cashmere. Baines eyes got wide. Correctly, remembering the police code, he roared into his walkie talkie. "10-32, 10-32." He said, "Put the fucking gun down."

"You're under a-fuckin-rrest." Williams spat, knocking Cashmere to the ground. Meanwhile Greer mushed Marco to the dirt, restraining his hands behind his back.

"Fuck off me." Marco drooled at Greer's feet, disrespecting his authority.

Attending to mind Cashmere lying beside him, gook caked around their mouths. Cashmere spit.

"Fuck these niggas bruh." Slaver, dribbling out of his mouth. "We dropping the dime on these pussies." He glanced back at the man laying ten feet away from him. His eyes were wasted and lifeless.
(Slow Motion)

Finley walks over to the breathless man. "I need a coroner to Garfield Park." He speaks into his walkie talkie. "I have a D.O.A."
"10-4." Said a voice on the other end of the device.

Nine and a half minutes later the ambulance came speeding through the park. Their tires imprinted on the grass throwing back mud waters into Cashmere and Marco's faces. Williams and Greer laughed to no end at Baines, who went to sit in the car like a bitch. His first day on the job, but sooner than he knew it, he'd become a crooked cop, cutting deals, making bribes just like the rest of them. It was only a matter of time.

EXT. Evening- Kedzie Ave 7PM

Cashmere was mad as shit. Fucking around, tussling with that cop got his sneakers dirty as hell. "Fuck bruh." He licked his finger trying to clean the mud off his LeBron's. "I should have dunked that nigga on his head twice. This whole outfit plus my kicks was ma fuckin two hunnit dollars bruh." Marco stopped at a parked car to check himself in the mirror. His eyes were red, irritated from the dirt that got in them.

   "Imma be on Greer's ass like white on rice. He's lucky I ain't shoot his bitch ass." (Yelling)

   "Cashmere, Marco." Alexis howled from across the street. Cashmere looked back at his mother. She wasn't even pretty anymore. Her face looked as if she hadn't washed it all week. The stench of her underarms raced to Cashmere's nose, nearly giving him a heart attack. She wore black leggings, old Timberland boots, a wife beater without a bra and a black bubble coat. "Hey son." She said yawning, blowing her breath out into the air. "Where the fuck y'all lil ninjas going?" She asked. "Y'all want some weed?" It might as well have been Christmas for Marco. "Hell yeah I want some smoke." He laughed.

"You know I get lit." Observing Alexis's outer presentation, Marco catechized whether she was alright or not. Her eyes had enough tax on them to last a month. Her complexion inhabited nothing more than being pale and ashy. "G-mom you looking rough." Marco coughed at the distasteful essence of her. "You aiight?" He asked. Alexis snarled, lighting herself a Marlboro cigarette. She inhaled that nicotine like it was the best thing on earth.

"I'm Gucci baby." She scratched her vagina through her droopy leggings. "Quinn's gone, take care of me." She glimpsed him hooking her up for a treat with some wealthy white man Todd. Cashmere's eyes just about dropped out of his sockets. As he's looking at Quinn signaling for his mother's attention his blood begins to boil. His pupils turned to iron. His fists loaded with anxiety.

"Marco gimme ya gun."

"Nigga for what?"

Marco didn't see what Cashmere saw.

"Bruh just gimme ya fuckin gun." Cashmere hollored. At first Marco didn't fathom what was going on. He was employed by checking out a shawty with red hair, a Jean dress, and red boots up to her thighs. "Aye bruh." Cashmere snapped. "Stop playing and gimme ya shit." He says, keeping his eyes on Quinn. When Marco realized what was going on, he openly passed Cashmere his .22

"Oh you know I'm with the shits."

(Indistinct Chatter)

"You want me to buy this hoe walking across the street?" Todd gapes out of his car window laughing. He wouldn't touch Alexis for fifty cents. He looked at Quinn like he lost

his ma-fuckin mind. Alexis on the other hand thought she hit the jackpot. She hurtled her way up to the car smiling, puffing on her cigarette. "She smokes?" He said watching her drag on her cancer stick.
"I don't do women that smoke." He bit his lip.
"Yeeaaa." He grunts. "I'll need that cash back buddy." He popped the armrest retrieving his 9mm laying it in his lap. Quinn flagged Alexis to stay put while he figured things out with the Paul Walker lookin ass dude.
"To bad homie. Quinn doesn't refund baby boy." "Uh huh." The guy cocks his gun back.
Meanwhile here comes Avah. She knew she'd find Quinn's ol stupid ass on the ave. She sashayed toward him when the gunshots went off. She saw the love of her life's body fall to the pavement. Alexis grabbed Quinn's .22 bucking at the guy's car.
(Bang)(Bang)(Bang) The car swerved all over Kedzie Avenue, the tires screeching until it lost control, crashing into an abandoned house. Both Avah and Alexis ran over to Quinn. Avah fell down beside her husband, crying for him not to die on her. "Avah I--" His breath shortened. "I love you." He caressed her cheek. "I'll always love you." He murmured.
"I love you too baby." She cried hysterically. "I love you too."

Seeing Alexis hurdling over her, she jumped to her feet, Quinn's blood on her hands. "Why are you here?" She screamed, slapping Alexis across the face. "Stay away from my husband you tacky ass bitch."

"He's my nigga to." Alexis spat. "Yup." She sucked her teeth. "He takes care of me."

"Tuh." Avah rolled her eyes. "Whatever hoe."

"And."

Alexis burped, scratching her dry scalp. "We have a baby on the way." She blurted out tapping her foot on the cement.

"Yup nigga." She stared down at Quinn. "You the daddy." (Silence)

While Avah and Alexis were going at it, Cashmere and Marco hit Todd's secret spot. They drew away his wallet, silver Rolex, credit cards and everything. Marco wanted cash. He double checked the armrest. BOOM!! There it was crisp one hundred dollar bills rolled up in rubber bands. Marco bewitched all four rolls of the loot putting it in his hoodie. Todd on the other hand groaned, suffering a bullet wound to the back of his head. Blood gushed from his head turning the collar of his white shirt to a crimson red color. Due to the nature of the scandalous infraction at any given second Finely, Williams and their two sidekicks, Greer and Baines would come rolling up on Kedzie Ave like big bad wolves.

"Aye bruh." Cashmere snatched Todd's silver chain off his neck. "You know the narcs about to pull up." He says, dropping the chain in his pocket. "Fuck is you looking for?"

"Nigga." Marco retorted. "I'm looking for the bag."

"Bag of what bruh." Cashmere asked. "We got the money. Let's go."

"Nah." Marco smirked. "I want everything this uppity ma fucker got."

He dug around on the floor beneath the passenger's seat. Walaa. Just what Marco was searching for. A sandwich bag full of coke in it. The white substance shined ever so

bright. It had to be worth at least three hundred dollars.
"Ching ching." Marco laughed.
(Cop Sirens)
   "Shit." Cashmere spat. Him and Marco both ran into the abandoned house. They raced side by side tripping up the broken wooden stairs. Finley, Baines, Greer and Williams arrived just as Cashmere and Marco took off running. Williams used his cro bar, ripping the car door off.
"Urgh." He growled. "Baines check him." Feeling almost inadequate to his partner, Baines didn't move a limb. Williams hollered. "What?" He said, "Are you scared of dead people?" He whispers, staring Baines in the eye.
   "No sir."
   "Get your dick outta your ass and search the mother fucker."
   The silent bark in Williams' voice sent chills up Baines spine. He started with the front seat of the 1960 red Cadillac. He slid his hand over every crevice discovering nothing of value.   "Sir there's nothing here." Said Baines. Williams smacked on a toothpick, killing time, waiting on Finley to come outside. "Keep looking." He said.
   "Sir I think he was robbed blind."
Williams burst out cackling. "Greer you hear this shit." He giggled until his ribs were aching.
   "I hear him." Greer chuckled. Suddenly his smile expired. His demeanor was vain and fierce.
"You are playing this good cop thing a little too well." He breathed, sneering in Baine's face.
"You wanna survive out here?" He instituted, panting down Baines throat.
   "Ye--" Baines stuttered. "Yes sir."
   Greer flicked his lighter, lighting himself a Salem cigarette. He takes a ten second drag, exhaled, smoke

exiting his nostrils. "Then fucking act like it." He says plucking the ashes of his cigarette on the ground.

INT. Cashmere- Finley & Marco

Lurking in the dark, a flashlight in his left hand, his nine millimeter in his right crossed over his left, Finley slithered through the forgotten house, inquiring for Cashmere and Marco.
Pussyfooting across broken glass, he kept his pistol out in case he had to shoot. He moved slowly, walking up the squeaky stairs. His flashlight guided him.
 "I know you lil mother fuckers are in here." He yelled, chuckling
 Cashmere and Marco held their breath. In less than a second, they burst out of the attic and tackled Finley's ass right to the floor full of dust particles and crack pipes.
 "Homie about to feel some fire." Cashmere said.
 "Damn." Marco whispered laughing. "You are a real killer now."
 "Yep." Cashmere replied. "These cops don't play fair." He uttered. "Why the fuck should we?"

Finley shined his light up toward the ceiling. Noticing a brown face through the cracks and crevices; that's when he heard gunshots and the other, a clamor of an explosion and a bullet to his upper body. He gasped for air pulling the trigger on his nine millimeter. Stumbling backwards into the wall, Finley felt blood oozing from his chest. He crawled down the stairs, covering his wound with his hand, the burning sensation rippling through him. He made it to the front door where fire ignited the Cadillac. A cloud of smoke polluted the air, dark flames growing higher toward the sky. Shattering glass was now the new song of Kedzie

Avenue. Neighbors scattered to safety as they saw the flames rising above their heads.

EXT. Car on fire-Fire Trucks- Back-up Police

"God...dammit." Williams murmured, briefly sprinting to Finley's rescue. "10-33." He said, "10-33.
 I need paramedics to Kedzie Avenue now." He shouts, grating his teeth. "Finley got hit, I repeat." He says, out of breath. "Finley... got...hit."   "10-4." The dispatcher replies. "Hang tight."   A fuzzy noise came over the walkie talkie.
 "I'm sending all units to you as we speak."

Finley glared at the fire in a rapid oxidation as he hit the ground. It almost felt as if he were the one being burned alive. The bullet had exploded through him. His entire life flashed before his eyes. Especially the day he married his gorgeous wife, Jianna. She was everything a man could want. She had beautiful honey brown skin, chinky eyes and she absolutely loved basketball. One of the reasons Finley doted on her so much is because Kobe Bryant was both their favorite basketball player. On their first date Finley took Jianna to a nice Japanese restaurant called Ichiban. Jianna wore a Lakers jersey dress, showing off her long cinnamon legs. Her jet black hair flowed naturally down to her elbows. Laying in Williams arms on that ice cold pavement, not knowing whether he was going to live or die, Finley made up his mind that he was going to tell Jianna everything about the stolen drug money, the illegal properties he purchased. The offshore accounts he had overseas. And the supposed to be business trips he took to L.A. was him pimping women on Skid Row. But he wasn't the only dirty cop. There were plenty more just like him.

Chapter #5 One Week Later Tuesday

INT. Morning-Laundry Room

Finley opened his eyes to the morning light greeting him as if it were an emergency. His colleague Greer, heavy on his mind. He rubbed the sleep from his eyes imagining the new face Greer would have after getting his plastic surgery. Fire had been burning in Finley's dreams ever since the explosion. The only thing that brought him back to reality was the smell of vanilla detergent. Climbing out of him and Jianna's king sized bed, Finley treaded toward where the lovely scent was coming from. There, he laid eyes on his soulmate. Watching her do her daily house duties as a wife made loving her easier everyday.
 "Baby."
 Finley tapped his fingers on the wall as he watched Jianna gather their laundry, dropping it into the washing machine. She bent over in her boy shorts to pick up a sock that had fallen on the floor.
 "My sexy husband." She blushed. "You are so damn fine."

Her smile, the way she stares at Finley as if he were the king of Egypt, Jianna was totally in love with her husband. He was just as much, the music to her ears as she was the beat to his soul. Standing up to his chin the softness of her breasts against his body, she clutched their hands together. Her five karat wedding ring shining on her finger.
 "I love you Ya'lae."

His heart began to speed up, the thumping in his chest beating.

Jianna poured two cups full of lavender and vanilla detergent. In a circular motion, she swirled it around on their clothes. She put the top on the detergent placing the bulky jug over top of the washing machine on the shelf. The stretching of her frame had Finley's eyes frequently glued to her hips and thighs. He took steps across the tiles, gliding up behind her. He held her at the waist, kissing the nape of her neck. There was a freestyle motion to her that he adored, a pure aura of realness about her that says, she's happy with who she is as a woman and wife. "Babe." She spun around slowly, kissing him, forever connecting their souls for eternity. "Are you still soar?" She asked, gaping into his eyes. They glared at one another until tears began to flow from their eyes. In a moment Jianna found herself kissing her husband's masculine chest. Her voice is as sweet as a saxophone. "Because--" She seductively says, "I kinda want you to make love to me." She bites his bottom lip and pulls him further into the laundry room, shutting the door.

Finley loosened up, forgetting the pain of his battle wound. The touch of his hands on Jianna's belly awakened her love for him even more. Beneath her salty tears, she kissed her husband, flooding his emotions with hers. As she craved his existence, the one way she knew how to get her husband excited was to show him some skin. Her flesh had blown out of control. Soon after they were naked in front of each other. Obsessed with how he loved her, Jianna welcomed her sexy husband into her vagina. Before Finley, she'd only ever loved one other man. And Finley's characteristics were definitely similar to his, which scared Jianna to death, but more so made her happy. She never knew eternity until marrying him after their high school graduation.

  As his hands traveled the distance from her breasts to her thighs, so did his lips. Finley knew that it only took a few kisses on Jianna's neck causing her to crumble in his arms. Long stroking her against the laundry room door, Jianna's hands began doing some bidding of their own. They fell down Finley's back. Her head swam in ecstasy. Their one desire was to make each other feel as though the floor fell from under them. In a matter of time it happened. The hotness of Finley's breath on Jianna's lips. Then came the tender hair pulling. The kisses become more intense as Jianna pulls Finley closer to her baby oil scented body. She moans in his ear.   "I love you big daddy. Make me squirt." She hissed. "Please." She begged. "I want to squirt on daddy's dick."

Finley's kisses are now in Jianna's hair on her shoulders. Already his intentions were to ejaculate a few babies inside of her. He squeezed his ass cheeks together and let it go. "Aarggh."
  He moaned, slapping her on the ass. "I fucking love you girl." He sucks on Jianna's lips as she squirts cream all over him. Their gaze lasted forever in a day, enough for them to know that they were truly each other's soulmates.

INT. Same Day- Noon

Jianna was folding clothes, the warm feeling against her hands relaxing to her mind, body and soul. Doing her husband's laundry was no red carpet event, but it brought her peace and tranquility. She loved the aroma of the crystal scented beads to tickle her nose. While laying out

Finley's uniform on the ironing board, a wrinkled piece of paper fell out of his pants pocket. Unfolding the paper, she saw that it was a receipt for an offshore account in the amount of 1.5 million dollars. Jianna gasped in shock, wondering what in the hell her husband was into. On her way to the living room to confront him about the large sum of money, she picked up on the tail end of his phone conversation. "You know me." He says, laughing, holding the phone to his ear.

"I'm a gangster out here. This uniform ain't nothing to me for real. Fuck you pay me." He snickered. "Feel me." On the other end of the phone was his partner in crime Williams, laughing his ass off. "I'm pimping hella hoes in L.A. this weekend too."

Jianna cleared her throat, startling the life out of her husband. He jumped, hurrying to end the call, but Jianna had already gotten an earful. And she heard enough. Her husband's words killed her life. In the furnace of the pain she felt, she couldn't extinguish what her and Finley's relationship would be like tomorrow or the day after that. The tears burst out of her eyes, spilling down her cheeks like water from a faucet. Everything she once appreciated in her home made her want to vomit. She's trembling and she can't stop herself. The walls that held her together for over ten years became weak.

"Jianna hear me out baby. Okay." Finley sighed.

"Um um." She sobbed. "I can't deal with you right now Finley." She walks away.

He grabs her by the arm. "Tuh." She shrugs.

"What the hell was all that about?" She quizzed him.

"You're a gangster?" She says, piercing him in the eyes. "Pimping hoes in L.A." She plucked his forehead.

"You took the oath babe." She screamed at him clutching him by the chin.

"To protect and serve." The tears are rapidly falling from her eyes. "Or did you forget." She slaps her thigh.

Little did Finley know it was too late for Jianna to hear or listen to anything he had to say. He spoke harsh words with the intention of letting Williams know that he was nothing but a crook in a blue uniform.

After those moments, Jianna uttered the very words that would tear her relationship apart. "I want a divorce." She says, crying in such a desolate way. Finley couldn't bear to see her losing herself. She went from happy to hanging on by a thread, a transformation that her husband himself could not change or reverse.

INT. Later that night- PM

Finley, and Williams were given specific instructions by captain Ruiz. She ran a tight ship in her department, or so Finley and Williams thought. Every now and then Ruiz would send them into the evidence room to make sure nothing was missing. The pallets near the wall to the left had a mass amount of cocaine wrapped in plastic on it. To the right was the money. Williams had a huge smile on his face. Meanwhile Finley stood there like a frozen silhouette. The aching words of Jianna wanting a divorce played in his head over and over again. He wanted so much to be close to her, laughing the way they used to. Instead he looked as though he escaped a horror film leaving behind its blackness. When Finley and Williams first walked into the room, Williams blood rushed to his head. His smile grew on its own as he touched the money. He couldn't hide it. However, he noticed Finley seemed out of it.

"It's all here man." Finley says, "Let's go." He began to exit the room.

"Let's go?" Williams laughed. "We can take some of this shit right now." He whispers, the silence in his voice getting deeper. "Ruiz won't even notice. Shit. Nobody would."

Finley broke the news to Williams as Williams was cutting through the plastic with his pocket knife. "She wants a divorce." He choked on his words, his hands on his hips. "She wants--" He punched the wall--"A fucking divorce." He huffed. "Can you believe that shit?" Williams dug out three stacks of money from the bottom right hand corner of the pallet. He put the money in Finley's hand.

"Go home." He says, "Jianna loves you.

She just needs a little time to cool off." Williams playfully slaps Finley on the arm. "Oh and not to mention." He says, tasting the cocaine. A warm chill came over him. He shook his shoulders as the narcotic shot straight to his brain. He nibbled on his bottom lip, grinding on his teeth. He stood still for a few minutes. The drug was doing its thing. His eyes became glossy. The room seemed as though it were going in circles. His thoughts slipped away from him.

"The wife-elect and I are having Sophia's birthday party next Saturday at four o'clock." He snaps his fingers together, gaining his memory back. "At our house." He says. "And you know how much she loves her godparents." This Finley knew.

"Yea."

He says, wiping the beads of sweat from his forehead. "Well." He sniffles. "Tell her, her goddad loves her." He pants. "Give her a kiss for me."

Sophia was the best goddaughter in the world. Her bright eyes were always so cheerful. Willow, her dearest teddy bear, barely hung by a thread. Sophia loved to chew on Willow's fluffy fingers. She'd laugh and tell Finley and Jianna that Willow wanted them to chew on her fingers too. Jianna had a strong weakness for Sophia. She catered to her as if she birthed her. To make Sophia happy, Jianna would pretend that Willow's furry fingers tasted like cotton candy.

INT. Saturday- Williams House

Sophia ran around the house, popping all of her pretty, colorful balloons after her mother Amber spent all morning blowing them up. When Amber wasn't looking Sophia kept on picking at the sides of her princess and the frog cake.
  "Sophia." Amber sighs. "Sophia leave the cake alone honey."
  Sophia dragged Willow, her bear by the arm. She swore Willow could talk and asked for a piece of the delicious cake. Amber chuckled at her humorous child.   "Honey." She says. "Bears can't talk."

Her sensational whisper came out followed by her lovely smile. Sophia got angry with her mother. She stomped her little feet. She gapes over her shoulder at her mother, who stood there laughing.
  "Willow can." She shouts.

 A knock at the door got Ambers attention. She figured it was Finley and Jianna, so she let them welcome themselves in. But when she saw the pair of feet, it was only one person. That one person was Finley. His face lit up as Sophia ran toward him. Amber smiled as well. Soon after, she noticed Finley was alone. She greets him with a hug and kiss.

"Muah. Muah." She puts a smooch on his cheek. "Where's Jianna?" Time works wonders. Because Williams walked through the door, a six pack of cold brews in his hand. Relieved more than ever, Finley faked a smile, exchanging a friendly hug with his partner and friend. Williams trotted along to the kitchen to put the beers in the refrigerator. Accept the one he kept out for himself.

"Where's Jianna?" He yells back at Finley. Finley scoffs under his breath. Then Williams realized why Jianna wasn't present. That changed in a matter of seconds.

"Hey god moms baby." Sophia raised her voice while embraced in Jianna's arms.

"I'm mad at mommy." She rolls her eyes, pouting her lips.

Jianna cracks up laughing, Sophia on her hip. She extends a warm hug and kiss to Amanda.
Sophia glared at her mother, batting her eyes at her. Amanda giggles.

"Don't you look at me like that young lady."

The fellas came out to the dining room, a couple of beers in their hands. Williams spoke first, greeting Jianna with a forehead kiss. She replied to his act of love toward her with a kiss of her own on his cheek. She completely disregarded her husband as if he weren't in the same room as her. Finley chugged on his brew. Still on duty, he couldn't drink but two or three. He's looking at Jianna who's totally giving him no attention whatsoever. He's gaping at how radiant she is in her red belly shirt. Her jeans tight as can be, ass shaped like a watermelon. Her butterscotch skin is glowing. He couldn't deny she had every reason to be upset with him. He wanted to explain. He calls her name, the tone of his voice mellow.

"Jianna baby." He says. "Can we talk?"

Amanda is steady setting up the table, adding plates, cups and napkins. Jianna gave her a hand picking up scrapples of plastic off of the floor. She brushed by Finley to put the scrapple in the trash. Finley trails behind her. He was making no progress in getting her attention.
 "Ba--" he says, but again Jianna dismissed him. Her Chanel perfume lingering as she walked by. The tension in the room began to rise. Finley drank the last of his brew. Once and for all, he attempts to explain himself to his wife.
 "Jianna." He says, "Baby we need to ta--" Jianna spun around. Her eyes bloodshot red. Her hands tremble.
 "I really cannot do this right now Finley."
 He shatters his empty beer bottle against the wall. Jianna jumped at the sudden noise.
"Goddammit Jianna." Finley hollers. "I'm trying to talk to you."

Amanda came rushing into the kitchen. Her heart crumbled in pieces seeing Jianna in tears. She didn't care about the glass on the floor. Her friend was hurting. Jianna sobbed on Amanda's shoulder. Her entire world felt as though it was falling apart. You see movies about crooked cops and drug dealers all the time. Never in a million years did Jianna think it'd be her and her husband's life.
 "Shit ain't sweet out there Jianna." Finley yelps. "I put my mother fucking life--" he grunts, "On the line everyday in them streets." He pounds his fists together. "I take bribes with drug dealers to stay alive." He yells. "There it is."
 "So quit Finley." Jianna threw her hands up.
 Finely bites down on his lip. His eyes get low. "You know what." He says, "Imma take your pretty ass out there. Imma' let you see what the fuck I go through."

Williams comes into the kitchen. A look of shock on his face. "Not just me." He looks at his partner. "The both of us." The tears kept on flowing. Amanda consoled her friend.

"Jianna baby." She says, "It's the life they live. She grabs her by the chin. "It's something we all live with."   "What?"

Jianna wept beneath her breath. "You knew about this." She muttered, disappointed.

"Jia--" Amanda says.

"Far as I'm concerned--" Jianna gapes at everyone in the room. All staring in her piercing brown eyes. "All of you can go to hell."

Sophia came running toward Jianna. Her footsteps no louder than a nickel rolling across the floor. Jianna embraced Sophia in her arms, stroking her bronze Shirley temple locks. "You know god mommy loves you right?" Sophia shook her head yes. Jianna pulls out a rectangular box wrapped in yellow gift paper. Sophia anxiously tore open her gift to a twenty four carat gold plated necklace with her name engraved. "Happy birthday baby." Jianna says, snapping the necklace around Sophia's neck. "But god mommy has to leave."

"I don't want you to go."

Her puppy dog eyes are as big as her birthday balloons.

Jianna gapes at Finley with sore eyes. She had nothing left in her to give. Everything about her marriage was based on bribes and dirty money. Knowing that Finley made deals with the same criminals, he was supposed to protect the streets from left a bad taste in Jianna's mouth. She unraveled her wedding band off of her finger laying it on the mauve countertop. A lump, the size of a boiled egg grew in Finley's throat. He might as well have been kicked in the stomach with a steel toe boot. He stared at the five carat ring that Jianna once cherished, lying there. It's as if the value of the ring went away.

   Amanda gasped at Jianna's decision.
"Jianna, sweetheart," she says, "You don't have to do this."

The touch of Williams' hand on Finley's back didn't help none. "Let her cool off man." He mumbles. Finley's heart shattered into what seemed to be a trillion pieces. He's looking at the ring. It didn't have the same meaning it did years back when he first proposed. There was an emptiness to it, a void he wanted to fill but couldn't. Jianna got her blazer off the coat rack, car keys and clutch bag, slamming the door behind her. Finley wanted to go after her. He loved her, but his job was way over her head. And if she didn't get it now, she never would.

EXT. Jianna- Night- Day 1

Outside of Presidents Lounge, a women's strip club on East 75th street, Jianna sat in her black Camaro, fatigue engraved on her pretty sad face. She stares at her ring finger. But there was no diamond to shine its light back at her. Her stomach gets queasy. And she feels a void in her heart where her husband used to be. She gripped the steering wheel, squeezing both sides of it. The leather feeling of it like a cushion on her forehead. She closed her eyes, but the tears made their way out, soaking her brown cheeks. (knock knock knock) Someone startled the hell out of Jianna. The girl standing there was no older than eighteen. Her attire spoke differently. Large gold earrings swung from her ears. She had on a black leather jacket that stopped at her waist. Her thighs thick in her denim jeans. Her nails were about five inches long. Beneath the parking lot lights, her brown skin glowed. Jianna rolls her window down a little bit. First thing she smelled was the girl's perfume. She had a fruit infused scent to her, the kind to linger when she walks ahead or away from you. Jianna got the perfect glimpse of the pretty caramel complexion female. She had a puma bag on her shoulder. Her cell phone on the other hand. It took a minute for Jianna to put two and two together before realizing the girl standing at her car was a stripper.

"Hi." She says. "I'm sorry. You don't know me." Her voice was frightening. "Do you mind walking inside with me?" The night hadn't grown old yet. There were a few cars in the parking lot, but not many. "I have a stalker." She explains. "And--" she bites her lip. "I don't want to walk in alone." Jianna shook her head yes.

"Yea." She sniffles. "I'll--" Her voice cracks. "I'll go in with you."

"I'm sorry if I caught you at a bad time."

"Have you ever been married?" Jianna wept to the stranger.

"I'm only 17." The girl retorts sharing a piece of herself. "My mom is--" she stops. "She's in my life, but she's not in my life you know what I mean. My father was murdered, so--" Jianna felt all the sympathy in the world for this girl. Seventeen years old with no one to turn to. And here she thought, she had it bad. "Are you alright?"

"I'm not." A broken Jianna replied. "I'm married." She pushes her bangs away from her eyes. "I shouldn't even be here." She snivels.

Jianna's style of weeping persisted of pearl shaped tears, flowing from her honey brown eyes. Her life crumbled at her fingertips. The steering wheel had become a pillow to her face. She gripped onto it wanting to scream. Nothing came out. The world she was most familiar with turned out

to be a blanket of fog. Her body became numb. She had no feeling and no proper thoughts about the life she'd been living with her husband over the last few years. Her reality darkened into carelessness. She's now gawking at the girl who's fiddling around in her purse. "Umph hmm." She clears her throat. An anxious smile spread across the girl's face. It appeared as if she saw God.
 "Ah ha." She sighs. "Found it."
 "Found what?"
 "Do you mind if I get in your car? I rather not do this out in the open." She chuckles. "Then everybody will want some and this shit is not cheap."

Jianna gave it a thought before unlocking the passenger side door. Once the girl heard the chirp, chirp sound, she walked around the car to get in.
 "I'm Reign Drop by the way." She says, as she retrieves a syringe and a small baggy out of her purse. "We can stay parked here or--" she squints. "You can pull up--" she nods toward a beat up shed, "right over there." A feeling the size of a penny bulged in Jianna's throat. This girl Reign Drop was preparing to shoot up and she wasn't afraid to show it. Jianna started her car.
Driving over the rocks sounded like someone was chewing on wood. She looks over at Reign Drop taking her jacket off. Her skin is dangerously scared with track marks starting at her wrists up to her forearm. Jianna stops by the shed. She cuts off the lights. Truth be told. This is what Finley meant when he said him and Williams took bribes to stay alive in the streets. But it was a few hours too late. Reign Drop exposed Jianna to heroin and what it felt like to fly high off that white.

INT. Night- President's Lounge

The scenery at President's Lounge was nothing Jianna ever seen before in her life. All the dancers walked freely in their stilettos half naked. Ass cheeks clapping on the stage. Random men throwing money at them. A white woman that looked like Velma from Scooby Doo, threw her ass back in some guys face. The crazy thing is, she wasn't all that attractive. Underneath her pale skin was acne. Her glasses were as crooked as a fork in the road. But she could shake her ass from here to Japan for some dollars. Reign Drop pulled Jianna by the arm. They went to the locker room where all the other girls were. Jianna gasped at the odor, keeping her hand over her mouth. Reign Drop paid it no mind. She was used to it. She sat her purse on the table. She rocks her head side to side thinking of a nickname for Jianna. She chuckles to herself. Her homegirl Double Dutch Donna giggles out loud.
  "I know your crazy ass done nicknamed her something wild," she says as she snorts a line of cocaine up her nostrils. "What is it?" She sniffs, adrenaline rushing through the veins.   "I'm gonna call her--" Reign Drop toys with Jianna's bangs. She slides her fingers beneath Jianna's. "Coconut." She leans back on the vanity table. Barbie spun around.
  "I'm so feeling that." She says while applying mascara to her already bold blue eyes. Their friend laughed as she slid into her performance suit.
  "Girl you like any and everything with yo white ass."
(Girls laughing)
  Reign Drop got Jianna acquainted with Peppermint Pattie, the coolest white girl ever. She especially loved some black men. You mention a brother in front of her and

she'll say, "how big was it" she always had the jokes. Jianna politely, but shyly smiled. "Girl." Said, Peppermint Pattie. "I'm not gonna bite you."

"She is lying." Donna laughed out loud. "And don't be fooled." She slapped Pattie on the ass.
"The bitch is crazy."

Jianna raised a shy brow. Her plain expression, solid on her face. The odor of coochie perspiration made her want to vomit. Obviously the other girls weren't bothered by it. "You all--" Jianna clears her throat, "Seems to be on a little something." She says, "No offense." She used the gesture of her hand when speaking.

"Girl you gots to be," says Barbie. "Crack will save your life." She nods at Donna. "Girl am I lying?"

"No worries." Donna snorkeled. "Barbie swear she's black."

In the moment of the ladies cracking jokes. Things got a little intense. "I may not be black," says, Peppermint Pattie who sniffed a line of cocaine as if it was nothing. "Umph." She gasped. "But I love a nigga wit--" the air in her lungs felt as if it was chocking her. She didn't mean to say the N word. Her skin crawled at the thought of all the black girls whipping her ass. Double Dutch Donna darted toward her. Reign Drop interfered or else Peppermint Pattie was gone get her ass beat.

"I didn't mean to say that." She frantically pleaded the fifth. "I swear I didn't."

Reign Drop looked at Jianna, who had no clue of what to do except stand there wearing a blank expression.

"Coconut." Reign Drop insisted. "Go to the bar and get yourself a beer." She retrieved twenty dollars out of her purse. "Tell them Reign Drop sent you."

"I--" Jianna stuttered. "I don't drink."

"Well." Reign Drop sighed. "Whatever." While talking to Jianna, she's steady, keeping a grip on Donna. "Get what you want and put it on my tab."

Jianna left the room. As soon as she closed the door, Double Dutch Donna was heard hollering. Glass bottles broke against the door. Jianna flinched at the noise behind her. Hesitant to go back, she went and sat at the bar. She skimmed through the menu to see what was good to eat. Her eyes grew big and wide when she saw the hot wing and fries specials. Being as though a lot of people weren't at the bar, she got fast service. The bartender wrote Jianna's order on a piece of white paper.

"I'll put this in for you hun." Says the pretty black girl with her thunder thighs bursting out of her tights. While waiting for her food, Jianna observed the females on stage, stroking the pole.

Chapter #6

INT. Night- Avah

It'd been two weeks since Quinn got shot on Kedzie Avenue. The first couple of days, he treated Avah as if she were the best thing that happened to him. He constantly communicated to her how much he loved her. How their daughter meant the world to him. Every single time, Avah fell for his bullshit. It all sounded so true and good at the moment. Quinn has this charm to him. He spoke sweetly to get what he wanted. And his sex. Lord that man could lay some pipe. Avah took advantage of Quinn being temporarily out of order. She walked around the house in a tank top and booty shorts. Her bare toes, brown and beautiful. Quinn stared at her ass as she bent over to water the plants in the living room. He sucked on his lip.

"Avah."

To hear him say her name sent chills up her spine. She secretly giggled before turning to him. She got a trick for his ol crippled ass.

"Yea babe."

"Come sit on daddy's dick."

Quinn laid the recliner chair back for Avah to climb on top of him. She's glaring at his physical appearance. At one point in time, Quinn was the most, sexiest man she'd ever seen. His eyes were powerful and gorgeous. His physique built well. Avah looked at him, thinking what went wrong. But she knew. It all started when he began drinking. He became physically abusive. He'd go out and buy her gifts, or cater to her with stacks of money. It worked for a while. But Avah realized, she can't be bought.

"Why Quinn?" She threw her arms across her breasts. "Your other bitch not answering her government phone." She stood there sucking her teeth. "You haven't had sex with me in weeks." She whispers, standing in eyesight of him. "I'm starting to feel like this is all a waste of time."

Her eyes began to water. Her voice got lost in between the emotions she was experiencing. There was an assuring tone in Quinn's voice. He wore a crooked, but not so convincing smirk on his face. It was more like a test to see if Avah would oblige to his demand. And she did hesitantly. She paced herself treading toward her manipulative husband. She gapes into his filthy, lying eyes. Knowing that he was fucking around on her with Alexis put a bad taste in her mouth. And to think, he impregnated the nasty heffer. Avah rises up. Although the bulge in Quinn's briefs got her juices flowing, she gasped for the strength not to fall for his tender kisses.

Quinn pulled her close. He kissed on her neck, smacked her on the ass.

"Go get me a soda from the store." His eyes went cold. "Please." He pretended to ask nicely.

Avah stood to her feet. It felt as though a brick fell on top of her.

"Something told me to leave your sorry ass--" She stuttered through tears, "To die on Kedzie Avenue." She wept. "But I didn't." She uttered. "Because you said you loved me." She threw a glass cup at Quinn's face. "This isn't love."

She shouts. Quinn blocked his face from the glass shattering on him. Avah got her pocketbook. She checked to make sure she had her I.d she had to get out of that house before she wound up in jail for first degree murder.

EXT. Night- Presidents Lounge- Cashmere and Marco

Cashmere already knew him and Marco couldn't get into the strip club. Especially since they were underage. The husky six foot four bodyguard stopped them right at the door. "I.d," was all he said. His fingers were entwined. His eyes hidden behind a pair of black shades. He wore army style joggers, a black beater and a small nose ring. His cologne lingered into the night. Marco stared the big guy up and down. Standing there, one hand in his pants, Marco rolled his eyes. Cashmere's hood covered half of his face. Only visible part of him was his lips. They were smooth brown. The bridge of his nose barely showed. His hoody fit his frame like a wrapper to a stick of winterfresh gum. His Hollister jeans are not tight on him. And his red slides are fresh, not even a speck of the dirt on them. While the bodyguard was busy requesting identification, the ladies absorbed the fragrance of Cashmere's Palmer's cocoa butter lotion.

Marco bargained with the security guard. "I'll give you a stack right now to let me and my man's in." It was the only way for them to get in. Marco dug in his pants pocket, pulling out a wad of money. Cashmere didn't even wait. He walked straight inside, Marco right behind him. "All I really want is some food bruh."
"Say less bro."
Marco rubs his stomach.
"I'm hungry as hell bruh."

INT. Cashmere Meets Jianna

Marco and Cashmere took a seat at the bar, about three chairs down from where Jianna sat. Cashmere looked over to her sad face. Him being charismatic, he cracked a smile. His bright white teeth shined even in the dim lights. His dimples accentuated his handsome, chocolate brown skin. Hesitant at first to speak, he mustered up the courage to make small talk with her. She accepted his warm energy with kindness while picking at her french fries. She dipped the fries in the cup of ketchup just to toss them to the side of her plate.
"Hmmiss." She sniffs as beads of tears escape her eyes. She buried her face in the palm of her hands.
"You could smile a little Ms." Cashmere says to her. "Can't be that bad." He's sitting there in all black, consuming Jianna with mysterious eyes. She stares to the right of her at him. Out of everyone in the lounge, Cashmere's scent came off more delicious than anything she'd ever smelled. Not to seem obvious, Jianna inched her nose in the direction of Cashmere. Suddenly, she wanted something sweet to eat. Intrigued by the bass in his voice, she gave him a subtle response.

"Would you smile if you were going through a divorce?" She ties her fingers in a knot, twisting and fiddling with them. Cashmere's smile faded away. "I didn't think so." Jianna wept.

Cashmere slid over toward her, sitting on the bar stool right beside her. As quick as his smile went away it came back just as fast. Through all the tears, he saw beauty in Jianna. Her spirit glowed. Her lips in the shape of a rose bud. Her top lip, medium thin. Her bottom one plush and sweet. She had the set of lips that curled at the rim of a drinking glass while sipping on a martini. Cashmere discreetly pulled five crisp, one hundred dollar bills out of his pocket wrapped in a rubber band.

"I hope your night gets better." He hands her the moolah. While Jianna's short conversation was coming to an end, Finley and Williams walked in. They're dressed in their full cop uniforms.
Jianna's heart nearly fell out of her ass.
"I really have to go." She hurries to her feet. "Thank you for the money." She says rushing out of sight. Cashmere kept his eye on her until she disappeared behind a curtain, leading to the ladies locker room. Talking about a short lived conversation, Cashmere joined Marco. Never a dull moment with him. Marco's ass done paid for a lap dance. This thotty ass stripper had her sweaty ass cheeks all in Marco's face, clapping them together. "Tuh." Cashmere chuckled. He bobbed his head to the music when he looked over his shoulder and saw Finley coming towards the bar.
"Aye bruh," says Cashmere. He nods at Finley. The bartender had just sat their plates down. Him and Marco immediately got up. Instead of eating their food at the

counter, they went to a table closest to the back of the lounge. Marco dipped his fries in ketchup.

"You think he saw us?" He asked.

"Nah." Cashmere glared at him. "He ain't see us."

As long as Finley was in the same room, Cashmere wouldn't dare take his eyes off of him. Every movement Finley made, Cashmere hawk eyed him like a lion would its prey. He hadn't taken one bite of his food. Meanwhile, Marco tore his jalapeno and swiss burger up as if it were school lunch. Beneath the table, he had his .22 clutched in his hand ready to pull the trigger.

Int- Jianna- Reign Drop- Locker Room

Reign Drop was in the middle of pulling her thong up between her ass cheeks. She was on in the next five minutes.

"Gimme a drink." Jianna demanded, pacing the floor beside her. Her nerves bounced around in different directions. She took one last peek into the lounge. Some nasty heffer was shaking her stinking ass all on Finley's dick. Jianna slammed the curtain closed. She cut her eyes at Reign Drop. "I want a drink." Her teeth grinding together. "And I want a drink now." She said. Her short temper turned into salty trickles of tears. Reign Drop got a bottle of Henny from her bag and a shot glass to go with it.

"Girl," she says, sitting on the edge of her own personal vanity table. "Are you alright?" She asked, pouring Jianna a drink. The Henny splashed against the bottom of the glass. Every note of it, satisfying to Yadira's ear.

Jianna threw that shot back so fast it gave her an instant buzz. "Besides the fact that there's a triflin ass BITCH," she pointed toward the lounge, "Shaking her sweaty ass all on my husband's dick--" She slams her glass down.

"Oh," She sarcastically utters. "I'm just fucking peachy."

Her lips stung as the warm drink hit her tongue. "Gimme another one." She wipes what little bit dripped down her chin. "I need more." She begged. Five shots later, Jianna is tipsy and feeling like she wanted to let loose. "I wanna dance." She said.

There's a whole rack of thongs and shoes near the wall. Jianna picked through the hangers until she found something she liked. She came across a sexy maroon thong set, a whip to go with it and a white baseball cap.

"Can I wear thi-?" She spun around to Reign Drop staring dead in her face. She has a raspy kind of laugh. Her pinch like face is small and cute as a button. Her picture framed body, perfect on her.

"Yea." She says. "You can wear that."

Reign Drop remembered her first experience on stage when she began dancing at the lounge. It wasn't that she was nervous to shake her ass. Because of that, she was a regular at clubs on weekends. But to really get on a stage, clapping your booty in front of strangers you definitely needed something to get and keep you going. Reign Drop sat Jianna down at her vanity. She untied Jianna's hair from that tight behind ponytail. Although it was super cute. Reign Drop tapped her fingers on her cheek, deciding what to do with Jianna's hair.

"Do you like your hair curly or more straight?" She quizzed, massaging Jianna's scalp. Jianna shrugged her shoulders. Depending on her outfit, is how she wore her hair. Reign Drop figured with the thong Jianna chose, she should wear her hair straight. Double Dutch Donna came in as high as a horse on steroids.

"Reign Drop." She said. "You're up baby girl." She smacked her on the ass.

"She wants to dance." Reign Drop smiles.

"Oh really?" Donna asked, surprised. "I'll fix her up."

"Thanks girl."

Henny had completely hit Jianna. She felt good and woozy. She pleaded with Reign Drop and Donna to let her go on stage first. She quickly changed into the set Reign Drop told her she could wear. She freshened up her mascara, drew on some red lipstick and buckled up her shoes. Reign Drop had some moose on her vanity. Jianna grabbed it, squirting some of it in her hand. She massaged it into her hair giving it some bounce.

"Well Zzamn." Donna laughed.

"How do I look?" Jianna stood to her feet. Her flawless complexion "Is it too much?"   "Hell no it's not too much." Reign Drop laid a line of cocaine out. "Do this first before you go out there."

Jianna was skeptical at first. Her heart sped up to her throat. Her fingers trembled. Suddenly, she found herself in an undesirable place. The lights appeared to go dim. Her eyes grow weary, reminiscing past experiences. *(Flashback)*

Jianna remembered herself walking home from cheerleading practice. She's laughing with her friends, Kiley and Kenzie. Kiley's teasing Jianna about her having a crush on Finley.

"Jianna we know you like him." The voice of Kenzie, clear in her thoughts. *Jianna went to put   her key in the door, but realized it's partially open.*

Tears cascade from her eyes, the horrible memory of finding her mother lying on her back on the living room table, unconscious, haunts her till this day.
(Flashback)
 "Ma."

 Jianna says, under her breath. Everything in her mind took place to her slowly walking toward the living room where she found her mother. *"Are you home?"* She remembers asking. Taking part in the exact same thing that took her mother's life, Jianna applied pressure to her right nostril, snorting the cocaine with her left one. The feeling of it gave her a rush to her temple that seemed to be good at the moment.
(Flashback)
 Jianna ran to her mother, screaming, "Ma please, no. Wake up."

Obsoleting that scary day, Jianna double checked herself. Seeing that she looked good, eyes glossier than a glass door, she strutted to the stage in confidence. The first person to lay eyes on her was Williams, Finley's partner in crime. He smacked Finley on the arm urging to go somewhere else. Finley was having the time of his life. Peppermint Pattie tossed her ass all up in his face. He threw five dollar bills at her. They were falling to the floor as she danced. The song changed and 'No Love' by J. Cole came on. Jianna gripped the pole with two hands. She began grinding her pussy on it. The steel rod rubbed back against her twat.
 "Lord have mercy." Williams muttered. Finley finally looked up. His eyes damn near rolled out of their sockets.

"Is that who I think it is?" He asked, knowing the answer to his own question. "Williams, is she fucking serious man?"

It wasn't the pole that Jianna was working. She gave the fellas something better to look at. Her limbs were in constant motion. She twirled her hips to the part of J. Cole singing, 'Believe we had a great night, but I ain't the type to tell you that I miss you' when he sang that next line 'After sexing on the floor' Jianna had wiggled and winded her ass out of the thong she was wearing. She held them at her fingertips before letting them hit the floor. She had Williams eyes bulging from his head. He licked his lips as he tried not to sexualize her. He was seconds away from going in his wallet to retrieve that one hundred dollar bill and toss it at her feet. Meanwhile, Finley was steaming mad. He pushed Peppermint Pattie out from in front of him. "Bitch move." He angrily growled at her.

He hastened his footsteps toward the stage. "Jianna I swear to God you better get the fuck off that stage and go put your fuckin clothes on." He roared.

The stage gave Jianna an outer body experience. Everything was blurry, but she could still see enough to know that men were loving her naked body. She climbed down off of the stage, pushing Finley backwards until he fell onto a chair. She sat on his lap giving him her bare self in front of the entire lounge. "You gonna arrest me baby?" She kissed his sweet tasting neck. "You're a bad boy Finley." The whispers of her soft voice caused Finley's dick to rise in his pants. "You can protect me can't you?"

Jianna nibbled on his earlobe. "Protect me like you do everyone else. Save me daddy." She plunged him into a French kiss. The Henny on her breath is warm. J. Cole's song came to an end. 'No love, No Love, No Love, No Love, No Love.' Jianna stared at her husband. She left him sitting there with blue balls. "Don't wait up for me." She said. Him and Williams didn't leave right away. In fact they decided they'd stay and have themselves a couple of shots.

INT. Avah Meets Jianna

By the look on Avah's face, it was obvious she was a woman scorned. Guys attempting to get her number, she pushed away. Fed up with men in general would be an understatement. She sat at the bar sipping on a bottle of water. Everyone else seemed to be enjoying themselves but her. This time there were more naked women walking around than before. Avah glanced at her herself in the mirror to the right of her. Her reflection had lost its glow. Not only was her skin bruised, but her body and her soul was hurt. Her aching heart cried for Quinn to stop beating on her as if she were a punching bag. Avah scanned the crowd for someone to talk to. "Ugh." She sighed, annoyed. Then she saw Jianna, an innocent look on her face. She felt comfortable enough that if Jianna sat next to her they'd converse and possibly have a drink together. Jianna plopped up on the stool. She was high as a kite. Eyes bloodshot red.
  "Henny please." She politely said.
  Peeping Avah sitting all alone, she spoke. "You're drinking water?" She asked unbelievably, "In a strip club?" Her graceful tone brought a smile to Avah's face. "Girl you better get a shot of something."
  "I'm not a big drinker."

"And I never danced or did cocaine until tonight." She shrugged Her shoulders laughing. "Shit happens." She smiles. "I'm Jianna."

"Avah." She says, getting acquainted.

In her opinion, Jianna was way too beautiful to be high on snow, but hey, the world people live in, drugs are everywhere, everyone is doing them.

"You don't have to sit over there by yourself." Jianna smirks. "Come sit with me. I'll get us both a drink."

The two ladies stayed at the lounge all night long. Somewhere after a few hours it was now 5am. Avah flipped shit.

"Omg." She says zipping up her purse. "I have to get home to my husband."

Quinn was going to beat Avah's ass. Jianna didn't give two fucks what Finley had to say about anything. As far as she was concerned, she didn't have to respect him. After all, the truth is, he's just as reckless as the criminals he puts in jail. As much as Avah tried hiding her scars, Jianna noticed them. They were on her neck. Handprints engraved around her wrists. It didn't take a FBI agent to know that Avah was being abused by someone. Jianna wasn't there to judge, but she damn sure disagreed with men hitting on women. Period!!

"Don't go home to him Avah," says Jianna. Her words are slightly slurred. At the same time there's truth in what she's saying. Her words come out poetically like she's humming a song. Clearly, she knows what she's talking about.

"You'll regret it later."

"Honey, it's not that simple." Avah wept. "We have a daughter, Adina. She's fourteen." She huffed and puffed.

"And dating." She chuckled a little bit. "Can you believe that?"

She retorted, envious of her daughter's relations with Cashmere. Jianna giggles. "No." She sips her drink. "I can't." She laughs, remembering her mother's rules on having boyfriends.

"I wasn't even allowed to look at boys until I was sixteen." The smile on her brown face accentuates her features.

"Then I met my husband." The cut off in Jianna's voice expressed loud and clear how she used to feel about her husband. She loved Finley with every bit of her. Things were just so different.

"Then I met my husband." She utters, sobbing.

Being the godmother of Sophia, Jianna could relate to where Avah was coming from. Because she loved Sophia as if she were her own child. Whole time, Cashmere never once took his eye off of Jianna. He barely recognized Avah until she looked in his direction. The structure of her face is what stood out to him. He had a recollection of her high cheekbones. Her somber eyes were somewhat dreary. She kept staring, thinking to herself, she'd seen Cashmere's face somewhere before. Then it dawned on her. He was the grandson of the woman whose house she went to, trying to find her daughter. She paid no mind to him at all, but wondered why in the hell he was sitting in a strip club.

Jianna snooped over her shoulder to see what and who Avah was looking at. She noticed it was Cashmere, the handsome young boy who sweet talked her earlier at the bar.

"You know him?"
"Something like that." Avah aforementioned. "He's too young to be up in here." She scoffs. "I'll tell you that much."
"Let's get out of here. I wanna go to the casino."
"It's late." Avah sighed. "I should get home."
Jianna couldn't help but roll her eyes. She bawled her fist into a knot, using it to hold her head up. Her right leg gracefully rested over her left one. She got the bartender's attention.
"Jack Daniel's please."
The bartender reached for the bottle behind her. She popped the cap off of it, pouring it in a shot glass. On accident, she automatically reached for a lime.
"Oh." Says, Jianna. "No lime please, thank you." She nursed her beverage taking one and two sips at a time until it was done.
"You're a gorgeous woman Avah, you deserve better."
"I know." Avah began to weep hysterically. "I know, it's just so hard to let go." She wiped her eyes. "I love him--" She snivels. "So much. We've been married a long time."

(Music Playing)

INT. Cashmere and Marco

Cashmere and Marco remained in the cut. They didn't care too much for all the ass they'd seen in a matter of thirty seconds. Their focus was to keep eyes on Finley and his sidekick, Williams.
Anything that popped off, Williams had Finley's front and vise versa. Every few minutes, Cashmere gazed at Jianna. Adjacent from his view, the rear of her lips stood out in his eyesight. Her posture upright just as a queen should be. There was meaning behind the gesture of her hands as

her lips perpetually moved. Two women talking, Lord knows what the conversation was about. From beneath his hood, Cashmere marinated in Jianna's presence. Her beauty was out of this world. He didn't wanna fuck or nothing like that. Shit, she was probably old enough to be his mother. But she was definitely a sight for sore eyes. Marco laughed out loud while breaking up a dime bag of weed in his lap.

"Thirty or not." He jokes. "I'll still hit that." He rolled over in his seat laughing. "Bruh you a nut." Cashmere chuckled.

CONTIN..

One and the other were in the same situation with the men in their lives. The men they gave their hearts and last names to at such young ages. It was much easier said than done in Jianna's case. Her and Finley did not have any children of their own. Whereas, Avah has a daughter. Jianna retrieved a napkin from the counter. She wiped the tears that were cascading down Avah's brown cheeks.

"It's gonna be okay. I promise." She hugged Avah as tight as she could. Stripping isn't for everyone. But it damn sure was the start of Jianna and Avah's tie-in.

Chapter 7

EXT. The Riot- Early Morning- Day 1

Neighbors swarmed the block of Kedzie Avenue. Apparently, a riot broke out in part of them protesting, to remodel the abandoned buildings rather than to tear them down. Supposedly, the city council also wanted to destroy the street Elliana Jean resided on and build condos for the upper class, rich white folks. Rose Bud, a elderly West Indian woman and her husband Hendrix have lived in their house for over thirty five years. They've all seen homes that were once beautiful, decay right in front of their faces. Every resident in a two mile radius either owned their property or were long time renters. They held up signs yelling. "No. No. Remodel Kedzie Avenue. Remodel Kedzie Avenue."

   Elliana Jean refused to have her home taken from her by the mark of the beast. With her husband gone, the house was all that was left of him. Davina came out on her front porch, rollers in her hair as usual. She banged on Elliana's door. Once she got inside, she went into the living room, where she found Elliana sitting in her rocking chair, knitting a set of bedroom curtains.

  "I ain't going out there." Elliana tells her.

  "Now you listen to me."

As Davina is talking to Elliana, she's tightening one of her rollers. Her brittle fingers shake.

  "This is our neighborhood too." She sits across from Elliana throwing a blanket over her lap. "Now." She says. "Do you mean to tell me--" She squints. "You're gonna let them take our homes away from us?"

  "Trust me when I say," Elliana assured her dear friend. "I am just fine."

By just fine, a man knocked on Elliana's screen door. She slowly made her way to greet Renzo. "How you doing Mrs. Jean?" He dropped off an envelope as instructed. Elliana knew exactly what it was. The sixth of each month, she received a stream of checks for businesses she owned. Cashmere never knew about any of it. Elliana made sure to keep him out of her street affairs. As he got older it became easier. Because he was too busy now,

ripping and running the streets with Marco. But boy was he in for a surprise. Meanwhile people were screaming, yelling.
"We own our homes. We own our homes."
  Cops were tackling them to the pavement, beating them with their crobars. With the good leg he had, Hendrix went out to his shed in his backyard to get his rifle. He returned to the living room ready for war. His wife pleaded against him going outside.
  "Hendrix baby, no." Rose Bud cried in her accent. "Them colonizers will kill you if you go out there." Hendrix practiced his aim. He looks at his wife, love in his eyes. . "Then let them kill my black ass." He cocks the rifle. "Our home is not for sale."

CONTIN...

Cashmere and Marco get to Kedzie Avenue. There's nothing but chaos and fire everywhere. "What the fuck." Cashmere says, muttering under his breath. He scans the block. He's looking at the cops. They're looking back at him. He realized he had nobody but Marco and his grandmother out in these cold streets. They walk through the fog, coughing. Cars are up in flames. In the midst of arms swinging, people fighting off the police, Cashmere felt a lump in his stomach. "NaNa bruh." He took off running. "Come on bruh." Him and Marco ran full speed around the corner. Their feet felt as light as a feather. Cashmere's heart is racing. Elliana and Ms. Davina were just coming off the stoop when he saw her. His heart dropped to the concrete. "NaNa you alright?" He asked out of breath. "You shouldn't be out here." He grabs her hand. "Where's your walker?"

"NaNa, Ms. Davina y'all good?" Marco questioned her second. "Hol up bruh." He tells Cashmere. "Before we bust any moves let me get NaNa her walker."

Marco grabbed Elliana's walker off the porch. He placed it in front of her. "Here you go NaNa."

Cashmere blurted out. "Marco let's go." He growls.

They ran in the house, skipping steps as they ran to Cashmere's bedroom. Marco shut the door behind them. Cashmere goes in the closet on the top shelf where he kept their black ski masks.

Marco raised his shirt. He kept a piece of steel on his hip at all times. "My nigga." Cashmere nodded. He tucked his .22 in the back of his pants. Him and Marco cover their faces. On the way downstairs, Cashmere noticed a piece of paper lying on the table. It was a check for one hundred grand and a five by seven envelope. From what Cashmere read, the check was signed by someone named Alessandro Esposito.

Attached to the check was the letter. It read 'Congratulations on your ownership over the President's Lounge, Mrs. Elliana Jean' The disturbing part of the letter was that Alessandro wanted Elliana to deliver two peoples' heads to him on a silver platter within forty eight hours for an additional three million dollars. Cashmere didn't have to ask his grandmother whether she'd do it or not. Because nobody in their right mind, a saint or not, is going to reject that amount of money. It was a matter of when she would actually do it. Just when Cashmere thought things couldn't get any worse, he finds out, not only does his grandmother own a strip lounge, but she's a hitwoman. "What the fuck bruh." Cashmere crumbled the letter throwing it on the floor.

"Aarrgghh."

He flipped the table upside down. "Damn man." BOOM!! He kicks the chair across the floor. Marco unscrambles the letter reading it for himself. His eyes widened reading the same information Cashmere had read just moments ago.
　"Yo." He said, scratching the bridge of his nose. "NaNa is really about this life."

Cashmere didn't have time to process anything else. Him and Marco ducked out of the back door down the alley. Paco's roof was the perfect place to get a good hit. Nobody would know where the bullets were coming from. Not even the cops. Cashmere and Marco climbed the rusted ladder, leading up to the roof. They found shelter twelve feet apart from one another. Cashmere shielded closer toward a red brick chimney. Whereas Marco covered up near a chipped wall leading down a set of steps to a door. In the darkness of the night, the only thing visible were their pupils. They stare at each other, signaling to make the first shot. From up above, the screams of people seemed infinite. The police are boundless to beat on anyone holding up a protest sign.
(Thudding Noise)
(Faint Footsteps)
　"What the fuck was that?" Asked Cashmere.
　He whispered low as could be, but loud enough for Marco to hear him. The steel in between his hands is fully loaded. He gripped it tight taking a peek at their extra company. As the footsteps became imprecise, Cashmere willingly qualified himself to pull the trigger. He observed the direction in which the person was going. "Three, two--" He utters, cocking his pistol back. "One." He says to himself. He ran up on the intruder as if he were skating on thin ice. The barrel of his twenty two pressed to the back of someone's head.

"Nigga don't move."

At the same time, Marco had come out with his gun drawn. Standing at least eight feet apart from Cashmere, he sighted the face in front of him as someone he and Cashmere both knew.   "Paco." He said, raising his mask over his lips. "The hell is you doing up here fool?" He lowers his gun. "We almost turned yo ass into oatmeal bruh."   Paco turned to Cashmere. And with a straight face.

"Damn bruh." He then chuckles. "You were really gone, put a bullet in the back of my head huh." He murmurs, nonchalantly.

"I was gone, blow yo shit off bruh."

Meanwhile, Cashmere has his eyes on the black duffle bag in Pacos hand. It could have been anything in there. More than likely, Cashmere figured it was cash, drugs and guns or all three. With Paco, you never really know what he's doing or thinking. He moves in silence. He never says much unless necessary.

"Bruh." Marco says. "You can't be doing shit like this."

"Whatchu doing up here anywhere?" Cashmere inquiries. More than caring about What Paco was doing on the roof, he purposely wanted him to unzip the bag. "What?"

He curiously wonders. "You gotta safe up here or something?" He anxiously questioned, pulling his mask up over his lips.

"That."

Paco retorted.

"And a couple of guns." He shrugs. "A OG like me gotta stay protected." He says, looking at
Cashmere and Marco, smoke breathing from the chimney. "Know what I'm saying."

EXT. Kedzie Avenue

People's outrage hadn't come to cease ever since it began at 6am this morning. Elliana's ears rang from the gunshots. Smoke in her eyes as she passed by dead bodies and smoke. Davina stayed right beside her, protesting, combing the block with their neighbors Rose Bud and her husband Hendrix.
   "This is our neighborhood." She shouts. "And we're not moving."
   Right then her life flashed before her eyes. Ahead of her stood a red neck white man, the word Nazi tattooed across his forehead in big green bold letters. He stared at both Elliana and Davina in their faces. The barrel of his shotgun pointed directly at Davina's temple. The smell of his breath and rotted teeth stung her nostrils.
   "We want chu NIGGERS out of here."
   "This is our home," says Elliana. "We're not leaving." She spoke as subtle as a child. Rose Bud held her by the arm. Davina on the other side of them. Tears streaming down their cheeks. Hendrix had his finger on the trigger waiting to blow the white Nazi off of his feet. The white man smiles evilly, and hawk spits on the ground at Elliana's feet.
   "Like I said niggers."
   He goes to pull the trigger, but the sound didn't come from his shotgun. It came from a cop standing behind him. As well as Hendrix's rifle. Both Rose Bud and the Nazi man fell to their feet. As soon as Hendrix saw his wife fall, he let off shots at every white person hollering nigger. He spun to his left. BANG!! To the right. BANG!! What made him stop was the blood seeping from his wife's abdomen. His heart grew weak as if someone pinned him to a wall for the fun of it. His eyes softened at the death of his wife lying on the ground in cold blood.

"Oh my sweetest angel." Hendrix dropped to his knees weeping. "My darling." He wept, rolling her onto her side. The oaky smell of gunsmoke burned his eyes. Tendrils of dust clogged his throat everytime he took a breath.

   Elliana and Davina were ambushed to the pavement, people trampling over them, yelling. Even after the smoke cleared, it stuck around, lingering in their faces.

EXT. Rooftop

Cashmere happened to look down into the crowd. He saw a white man holding his large weapon in his grandmother's face. She laid helpless on the cement with a gun at her. That was all it took. "Paco gimme one of your guns. Hurry the fuck up bruh." His blood boiled. Adrenaline pumped through his veins. Paco unzipped the bag giving Cashmere his favorite tool, the one with the lense on it holding fifteen rounds. Paco showed him how to aim it. How to stand in position to get a clear shot. Cashmere held the weapon up in black leather gloves. He closed one eye. He took a deep breath. BANG!!! He shot twice. BANG!! The pressure nearly knocked him off his feet. BANG!! Marco followed up, no explanation needed.

(Woman Screaming)

There wasn't an ounce of remorse on Cashmere's face after pulling that trigger. If anything, the happiness of killing someone who deserved it entertained him. From afar, he gaped at the white man's body. His face down on the pavement, blood leaking toward other people's feet. Cashmere fell into a trance. It felt as though his soul had gone somewhere to another dimension. The commotion of the riot was very much still intense. Flames grew higher, screams louder. Cashmere pulled his mask off. He's perspiring.

"Bruh." Marco turns to him. "One of us gotta go down there."

"I'll go." Cashmere insisted. "I gotta check on NaNa and make sure she's cool and shit."

"I'll stay up here with Paco and keep a check on the scenery."

"Nah." Paco disagreed. "Marco go wit em."

Marco's loyalty was never a question. "You know I gotcha back dawg." He says.

"That's what the fuck I'm talking bout," says Paco. "That's real nigga shit right there."

CONTIN....

Finely hadn't seen Paco since the shooting incident. Being the younger bad brother, he decided to pay his sibling a visit. Beforehand, he wanted to put his drugs and money in the stash. He moved as quietly as a mouse as he came through the door holding a brown leather briefcase. To his surprise his older brother stood before him. The look on Cashmere and Marco's face turned from warm to cold. Finley toughened up, spoke with his chest out. His instincts led him to believe that Cashmere and Marco were the faces behind the black masks. He treads up to Cashmere first pulling his mask off, throwing it on the ground. He chuckles to himself, nodding his head side to side. Cashmere raised his hand, the barrel of his gun in Finley's face.

"Something funny nigga." He says, nonchalantly.

Marco has his finger on the trigger of his pistol as well. He went shooting first and asked questions later. Had it not been for Paco, Finley's ass would have been hauled off of the roof on a stretcher.

"Long time no see big brother." Finley grinned, slapping his brother on the arm. "How's mama doing?"

"Chu' doing here Ya'lae ?" Asked Paco. "And you'd know if you called home more often."

Cashmere's eyes grew to the size of grapes. The grim look on all three of their faces was more deadly than it was friendly. Cashmere locked his eyes on Finley until he broke the silence. "Heard ya g-mom is the new owner of President's Lounge," he says, as he pops a piece of gum in his mouth. "Congratulations to her." He sarcastically jokes, clapping his hands sitting alongside of the brick wall. "Oh." He says.

"But you didn't know that I knew--" He gets in Cashmere's face chewing on a stick of trident gum. "Ya' g-mom is," He utters, his voice barely understandable, "The biggest crack dealer in Chicago."

"Ya'lae chill the fuck out man." Paco said.

By then Cashmere had already hawked spit in Finley's face. His adrenaline raced through his veins. He wished to God Finley would bust a move. The way he felt, Finley had a beat down coming. He gripped Cashmere up by his throat, wrestling him to the pavement. "The only reason you're lil bitch ass is alive--" He hissed in Cashmere's ear, "Is because of my brother. He pays me good money not to kill your punk ass." Cashmere wiggled as Finley used his police technique to keep him restrained. Cashmere was almost foaming from the mouth till he reached up pinching the pressure points in Finley's neck. Finley immediately released him, staggering to refrain himself from showing weakness.

"Argh shit." He said. He hears the click of a gun.

Marco stood there, no emotion on his face at all.

"And you lil nigga," Finley shrugged his shoulders back. "I want your ass on a silver platter."   He stumbles toward Marco knocking the pistol out of his hand.

"You're the one." He says, rolling his neck around to get the feeling back. "You're the one that shot me."

Marco smirked. "Nah." He giggles. "I didn't." The sly smile on his face fades. "But my nigga did." He nods toward Cashmere.

Finley scolded Cashmere, lunging at him as if he stole something from his momma. He dragged Cashmere to the wall of the roof hanging him backwards over it. Cashmere's mind raced at the thought of his body splattering, one hundred and twenty feet down to the cement. Expressing no fear physically, he relaxed himself, laughing in Finley's face. Finley pressed his forearm against Cashmere's throat. He croaked, gasping for air. In the rear of his eyesight, he saw Marco walking up behind Finley.

"I should toss--" Saliva spat from his mouth onto Cashmere's cheek, "Ya ma fuckin ass over this bitch." Finley says, gritting his teeth. "You'll just be another homicide that Chicago doesn't give a fuck about."

The menacing look in Marco's eyes were devilish. The features of his face behind the mask were just as evil without it. He raised his arm mid-length, biting his bottom lip. He squeezed the trigger. POW!! He shot a single bullet into Finley's thigh. Finley yelped in agony, the bullet penetrated, breaking through his skin. Paco had enough of them going back and forth, exchanging bullets at each other. He straddled Marco into a headlock. "Chill out young thug."

He says. "Trust me." The firm tone that came off of his tongue puts an apple seed of fear in Marco's heart. "This is not what you want."   Marco squirmed loose from Paco's grip.

   "The fuck off me bruh." He howled in anger. "Whose fuckin side you on bruh?" He hollered. "Huh?" He spat. "You with this clown?" He points at Finley. "Or you with us?" He yells. "You tell me motha fucka."

Paco breathed deep within himself, the rising in his chest masculine, the morning breeze exiting his mouth. "Nigga he said what side?" Cashmere perpetually yells. Marco shook his head, highly disappointed in Paco for not telling him and Cashmere that he and Finley were blood brothers.
   "Tell me that's not really your brother Paco?"
   Marco shows the hurt in his eyes. Embarrassed to admit the relation to his youngins, Paco stayed silent. In all actuality they were all thugs. One just happens to be in a blue uniform with a badge to his name.

Chapter #8

INT- Later That Day- 48 hours later

Cashmere still barely believed his grandmother hadn't given up the street life like she said she did. She may not be working the corners of Kedzie Avenue, bagging or cutting up the cocaine, but she owned the lounge, which meant she got a portion of all transactions. Thoughts of Elliana slanging coke boggled Cashmere's mind. Laying on his back, eyes to the ceiling, Cashmere's fantasies were disturbed by pebbles being thrown at his bedroom window. He climbed out of bed, grabbed his pistol from under his mattress, and peeks out of the blinds. With the riot going on, God only knows who was out there. Cashmere pulled the string, raising the shade. Adina had come to see him. She smiled up at him, biting her lip. He cracked the window just enough to tell her to hold on a sec, he'd come downstairs to open the door for her. When he did, Adina couldn't help but notice his abs. Her stomach fluttered, imagining him taking her virginity. She daydreamed of him kissing on her skin and biting her neck.

"Hey." She says, somewhat shy.

"Sup witchu'?"

He retorted, admiring her red and orange African headwrap and casual winter attire. She had on a white fitted shirt, faded blue jeans, rips up to her thighs, lime green shell toe shoes and a black pea coat. Her posture was of a Nubian Queen. Her flawless complexion glowed even on a foggy day. Her full lips are deeply moisturized.

"How'd you get here?" He questioned, leaning against the counter. Hesitant at first to make a move on him, Adina pressed her body against his. She began kissing the nape of his neck, loving the fruity, but masculine taste of his skin on her lips and tongue. Taking the time to answer his question between kisses, she replies.

"I walked."

"Through all that shit out there?" Cashmere muttered.

"

I

w
a
n
t
e

d

t

o

s

e

e

y

o

u

.

"

A whisper of love sparked in Adina's brown eyes, stemming from the depths of her soul.
 "You're wet."
 She gawked Cashmere in the eyes, emotional warmth transpired between them. Cashmere just knew the floor sunk from under his feet when Adina uttered, "I want you to be my first babe."   She said it with such confidence, alluring his hands around to her waistline. Cashmere slid his tongue across his lips at the feeling of Adina sucking on his sweet skin, caressing his manhood.
She got a hold of the shaft of his penis. She gushed at how swoll it felt in the palm of her hand.
Their eyes meet for what felt like the first time ever. There was a particular way Cashmere
looked at Adina. From the first time he saw that twinkle in her eyes to the dimples in her cheeks. At this very moment, Adina wanted Cashmere for herself. She wasn't at all timid to show him how she felt about him either.

Thunder seemed to race through her. She took her sweet time swishing her tongue around in Cashmere's mouth, the tips of her fingernails cascading down his spine.
"You know what you're doing?" He gasped in between their kisses, cusping her buttocks. He went on to pull her left leg up around his waist, squeezing her close. The fragrance of Adina's skin is subtle yet sweet.
"Um um." She uttered, steadily arousing him before vacuuming him into her seductive aura.
"Take me to your bedroom?" She demanded. "Make love to me Cashmere."
A girl had never asked Cashmere to take her virginity. He froze briefly giving in to her offer. Escorting her by the waist, he led her to his bedroom. His penis grew bigger as he prepared to fuck her guts out. No more than a second had passed. Cashmere had Adina jammed, up against the wall. He'd never looked at any other girl, the way he looked at Adina. She has sensual eyes, a heartwarming smile to go with it. As soon as Cashmere pulled her closer to him, her energy shifted, bringing butterflies to her stomach. The warmth of his breath tickled her nose, she just smiled. Quite fond of the structure of her chin, he raised her lips to his while removing her jacket. No patience at all, Adina nervously, but willingly slid out of her skin tight jeans. Face to the wall, she gapes halfway over her shoulder at Cashmere. His hands were already busy on her, his eyes fixated on the statue of her physique.
The feel of his index finger going down Adina's back raised the hairs on her arms. The smell of him from behind her moisturizing her thighs. He had a scent of honey and brown sugar mixed together. Cashmere dropped his boxers to his ankles. To him, Adina was different. He wanted to savor every part of her body. However; he couldn't discipline himself when it came to teasing her. He

gripped the shaft of his penis. With three of his fingers, he gently entered Adina's temple, touching the surface of her hyman.

"Ssss." She exhaled. "Umph." She moaned.

Cashmere could only picture how Adina was feeling. Afterall, he was blessed for his age. He pulled out an inch, applying pressure once more. This time Adina began to moan as Cashmere continued on at a comfortable pace. He clutched Adina by the shoulders, slow grinding in her pussy till his dick was submerged in her juices. He bit on his bottom lip, squeezing his butt cheeks together. Each stroke, thrusting himself deeper into her, but not enough to break her in.

"Imma marry yo ass girl."

He talked shit, kissing on her shoulder blades. So badly, Cashmere wanted to beat Adina's back in. Then he considered how amazing it'd feel having her legs draped around his waist, missionary style. He pulled out completely, turning Adina toward him. He reached for her hand, a sucker for love and affection, Adina grabbed it. Cashmere walked backward, Adina following his lead. She had no experience in oral sex, or sex period. What she did know is that

Cashmere's dick was beautiful. It was a nice solid brown, the head big and juicy. His pubic hairs were neat. Adina pushed him back onto the bed. She got on her knees prepared to snatch Cashmere's whole soul. His iron rod stared her in the face. She held it in her hand, tongue kissing, and slurping all over it. A few times she smacked her lips with it.

Cashmere arched his back, groaning. When she held her breath and started deep throating, the pressure of him ejaculating in her mouth became so intense his legs

quivered. Without even realizing it, his toes curled. He's panting, trying to catch his breath.
"Adina stop." He begged. "Damn girl."

She let out a chuckle like yea, I'm about to make his ass cum. On top of that his dick tasted like cotton candy. It didn't matter to Adina that Cashmere asked her to stop. Slobbing on his knob had her ready to fuck all night. She spit on his penis, goggling him up as if there were no tomorrow. "Umph." He gasped. "Shi--." He moaned, hissing. "Imma cum in your mouth if you don't stop doing that shit girl. I swear to God."
Adina spit on his dick one more time before she totally slurped the cream right out of him. A clear liquid oozed out of the shaft of his tool. He gripped the sheets in his hands, eyes rolled to the back of his head. Adina made sure to catch every drop of him on her lips and in her mouth. She smiled a smile of something great that she'd accomplished. Afterwards, she climbed into Cashmere's bed waiting for him to finish what she started.

CONTIN....

In the semi-dark room, Cashmere lingers over Adina, admiring the colors in her scarf, that she'd tied in a bun right above her perfectly arched eyebrows. Also bringing out the brown in her eyes. She might as well have been Oya, the goddess of love and light. He didn't linger too long, but intentionally wanted Adina to know that she was beautiful and that his hands would do everything else, that he couldn't say verbally. Through her shirt, he lightly nibbled on her nipples. She rubbed the top of his head. Her trimmed nails, relaxing to his scalp. It didn't take long for Cashmere to get her out of her bra and shirt. He slid up into Adina's thighs with ease. Meanwhile, she's gazing deep into his eyes. Her heart is rapidly beating. She can't shake the suave fragrance of Cashmere's scent. She wanted to taste him over and over again. She wanted every part of his body to touch hers. Cashmere gapes at her, meeting her lips with a kiss. At the same time, he's reaching for his shaft. Finding the opening to Adina's moistened vagina, he pressed himself against her hyman. She grabbed a hold of him, panting, and moaning his name. All the while, she's taking in the pain, along with the pleasure he was giving to her young and tender body.

INT- Cashmere and Adina- Casual Conversation

Adina knew in her heart from this day forward, she and Cashmere built a bond. No female after her would ever be able to compare to the peace Cashmere felt being in her presence. She laid comfortably on his chest, no worries in the world. She had one leg over top of his, resting her hand beneath her chin. Cashmere was exactly what and who she wanted. More importantly, she felt that she could trust him. Especially with the thoughts that were in her head.   "Baby." She says, whispering. "What if I wanted to rob a bank." She looks up at him. "Would you be down with it?" Her face, so innocent, but her voice, so serious. Cashmere smiles and licks his lips.
 "And I thought I was bad." He chuckles. "It's the perfect crime though baby girl." While talking, he's gliding his fingers up and down Adina's spine. A warm chill rushes through her, the sensation of his touch against her skin causes her to scoot closer toward him. While at it, she takes the opportunity to steal a kiss from him.

(Faint knock on the door)

Cashmere sighed. He'd been familiar with the sound of his grandmother's fragile hands for a while now. With everything that's been going on, he did his best to avoid her. Having Adina around, she didn't tolerate Cashmere disrespecting his grandmother.
  "It's probably your grandma babe." She says reaching for her shirt at the other end of the bed.
"Put your clothes on, and see what she wants."
  Elliana knocked on the wooden door again. Accept this time, the doorknob slightly turned. It was her pushing the door apart with her walker. Cashmere sat there, not bothering to lift a finger to assist her. But he noticed envelopes in her hand as she struggled getting in the door.
"You're so damn rude." Adina elbows him. "I should leave." She sprung to her feet. "H--" She stuttered. "Hi Ms. Jean. Cashmere and I was just about to go get something to eat." She looks back at him, rolling her eyes. "Did you want anything?" She offers. "I can get you a soup and a salad or something." Cashmere observed Adina's acts of kindness toward his grandmother.
  "You."
  Elliana coughs-- "Are too kind sweet--" She coughs again-- "Sweetheart." She finally managed to say, after struggling to put her words together.
Years of smoking, and drinking, turning up every weekend, Elliana now survived off of her oxygen tank. That's when she wasn't being hardheaded. She hated that thing. Walking around with it, attached to her walker annoyed her even more. She'd rather cough and choke than to lug that tank back and forth.

Meanwhile, Cashmere sees the envelope in her hand, he didn't know what it was. Figuring it may be money, he inquired. "What is it NaNa?" He asked. "What do you want me to do? I gotta deliver some drugs for you or sum?" The bones in Elliana's hand were deteriorating making it difficult for her to hold things for short, or long periods of time. Disregarding Cashmere's smart mouth, she turned to leave the room. Cashmere didn't stop her either. He didn't give a fuck anymore. That's how disappointed he was in finding out who his grandmother really was. He felt as though, the woman he knew her to be was all a front. He gawked at her taking baby steps toward the door. Adina stares at him. She folds her arms across her chest waiting to see if Cashmere would budge. He lay there in bed, his hand behind his head, staring up at the ceiling.   "We'll do it Mrs. Jean," says Adina. "Whatever it is--" She shot Cashmere a dirty look. "We'll get it done."

She retrieves the envelope, curious to know what's in it. "Nah."
Cashmere sprawls to his feet. "I'm about to meet up with my boy Marco."   "Yea."
Adina says, sincerely speaking, "After we take care of whatever your grandmother needs done babe." She pokes her hip out. "Marco can wait."

It turned Cashmere on, how Adina took charge at him. Aside from his grandmother, no other female spoke to him that way. He's getting dressed, pretending to ignore her, when really, he wanted to accelerate himself into her thighs, and eat her tight lil pussy. He's looking at her lips moving in what seemed to be slow motion. She's steady talking away to him. Cashmere sits on the bed, a sly smile on his face as he leans over to lace up his purple and white Converse. He checks himself in the mirror to see if his jeans match his footwear. He wouldn't dare leave the house unless his kicks were on point.

Satisfied with his swag, he grabbed his red, and black Chicago Bulls sweater from the closet.

As he's pulling the sweater over his head, Adina's staring his sexy ass down. Not only did Cashmere look good as hell, but the fragrance of blueberry, and vanilla seeped from his pores. Adina accidentally groaned out loud, biting on her bottom lip. Cashmere smirked, and seductively licked his lips while applying his cherry flavored Chapstick to his lips.

The grin on his face is so enticing. He pulls Adina close to him, gripping her at the waistline. He lifts her chin up to him, silently kissing her until she could no longer feel her knees. She's holding him by the elbows, reciprocating her energy, chills going up his spine. They meet each other at eye level and smile. After five minutes of Cashmere brushing his waves in the mirror, he put on his fitted Yankee hat, and was ready to go.

EXT. The Break In- The Bulldozer

The doorbell rang multiple times. Renzo stood outside, on the front porch, dressed in all black, waiting for Elliana to answer. He'd known her since he was a kid. He saw her work the streets of Chicago way back when. He even made a few drug runs for her. It would definitely hurt his heart to have to manhandle her in any kind of way. But she wasn't leaving him much of a choice. The only other alternative was his head on a stick if he didn't return to Alessandro with what he wanted. Elliana's only option was to comply or deal with the repercussions. Renzo reached in his pants pocket for a pair of black leather gloves, and something to pick the lock with. He got as close to the door as he possibly could. As he's fixing to break into Elliana's house using a heavy duty paperclip, Davina comes outside puffing on her Camel cigarette. She stares at Renzo. She smiles at him, not knowing what he was up to. A cloud of cigarette smoke escaped her mouth.

  "Hey there sweet pea." She says, exhaling before taking another long drag. At first her motherly demeanor was polite, and cheerful until she realized, Renzo's attire was more of a hit man. "Boy." She glanced at his hands, covered in leather. "What in the hell are you doing?" She quizzed him. "You best to leave Mrs. Jean alone." She fussed.

  "You hear me Renzo?" She points her cigarette finger at him. "That woman--" She scoffs, her cigarette burning in her hand, "Doesn't bother no-damn-body." Renzo almost got the door open, but Davina wouldn't shut her mouth. "Renzo." She says, pouting her lips into the shape of a ball. "I will call the police--" she grits her teeth-- "On yo ass."

At the mention of them boys, Renzo hopped over onto Davina's side of the porch. He yoked her up by the back of her neck, forcing her through the screen door. He dragged her inside of the house by her neck. He shoved her to the floor.

  "Make one move." He promised her. A menacing look on his face. "And I'll put a bullet--" he emphasized, clenching his jaws together-- "in the back of your head." He threatened. "Stay yo ass still."

Davina laid faced down on the floor between the foyer, and the living room. Her hands flat on the carpet. From the sound of banging noises, Davina was sure that Renzo was in the kitchen searching for something. She heard the clunking of her caddy utensils, a noise in particular that she prayed wasn't what she thought it out to be. She tilts her head up seeing Renzo's feet. He was coming toward her with duct tape, and a knife in his hand. Davina pleaded for him not to kill her. Her heart is rapidly beating as Renzo gets down on one knee.

"Renzo please." She wept. "I'm sorry." She gasps, shielding her face with her arm. "I won't call the police if you just let me go."

Renzo twisted her left arm behind her back. Then her right arm, unraveling the tape tightly around her wrists. Davina laid there as helpless as anybody could be. She tried to wiggle her hands free. Renzo took his pistol, knocking her upside the head with it, splitting one of her many pink rollers in half.

"I didn't want to do you like this." He pants. "But goddamn." He pounced to his feet.

"You just kept running your mouth." He sighed, lighting himself a blunt. "Now look at you." He inhaled the potent weed plant-- "Look what you made me do to yo old ass."

(Two gunshot sounds echo)

INT. Ellian Jean's House

"Mrs. Jean, Mrs. Jean." Renzo walked through the house calling her name. "I know you're in here." He's treading around the living room, looking at family photos. Making his way toward Elliana's bedroom, he kicked the door open to nothing except an empty space. There was nothing but silence. It was Elliana's favorite picture of her, and Jesse Jean on the nightstand, that caught Renzo's attention.

They'd gone to a red, and white, black love affair that weekend in Cali. Of course Jesse was dressed to kill, and with Elliana beside him, they definitely made a statement in their matching attire. Elliana wore a Designs By Shay, red midi dress that hugged her curves so tight, Jesse Jean almost declined her to wear it. Being the confident man that he was, he let Elliana get her shine on. As for him, he chose his white Fari X slacks, and a red blazer, no shirt underneath. He and Elliana pulled up in a black stretch limo. Boy, did they turn heads. Most of Chicago's other top hustlers made their grand appearances as well, pulling up in suburban trucks with their wives, and girlfriends.

Cali king pins were a breed of show offs. Nevertheless did they intimidate Jesse Jean, or Elliana. They were young, fortunate, and well respected.

Renzo held the frame in his hand. His eyes turned cold. "King Pin Jesse James." He says, spitting on the picture. "I never did like your pretty boy ass."

It isn't like Elliana could get far on a bad leg, her walker, and the oxygen tank. The bathroom door was the only door closed in the house. Renzo crept up against the wall, driving his foot into the door. The bathroom looked as though it hadn't been used all day. Tissue was positioned in its spot to a perfection. The his and hers glass mirrors were so clean, Renzo saw himself in them. Fascinated with the yellow decor, he grinned as he unzipped his pants to take a piss.

Meanwhile, Elliana is quiet as a mouse, sitting on her chair in the shower.

In the middle of Renzo zipping up his pants, a loud thud came from downstairs. Elliana Jean's house was being torn apart by a bulldozer. She couldn't help but sob behind the curtain. Her tears became hysterical enough that

Renzo snatched the curtain back with his pissy ass hands. There, he found a fragile Elliana holding an envelope in her hand. It was a thirty day eviction letter from the city of Chicago.

All residents were ordered to vacate a month ago. Apparently Fuller Park was being remodeled for rich white folks.

Renzo gawks Elliana in the face. "I don't wanna' do this to you Mrs. Jean." He says. "You know the ru--"

"This is--" Elliana blurted out, "my home Renzo." She croaked. "You can't--" she coughs, "Take me from my home."

Renzo didn't want to put his hands on Elliana. However, she left him no choice. She refused to come out of the shower. Even while her home was being shredded to pieces. Renzo forced her weak body over his shoulder. She's punching him, tears cascading down her cheeks. They get to the bottom of the stairs. Elliana's first glimpse was her living room. It was totally destroyed, shattered glass everywhere. Pictures of her and Jesse Jean obsolete. "Jesse Jean." She murmured as she wept over Renzo's shoulder.

Chapter #9

EXT: 4pm- Chase Bank- Adina & Cashmere

Chase bank, where the majority of Chicago's residents loved the company's coffee, and refreshment table. Nothing seemed unusual for them today. They smiled casually, chit chatting with one another as they waited their turn in line to deposit their checks.

"These riots are just absurd." Said a blonde, blue eyed woman to her friend in her Southern accent.

"I tell you what." She uttered. "It's mainly the colored folks." She gawks at the few black people who were simply minding their business. "They're all a bunch of heathens."

"You can say that again," says the other woman as Cashmere walks into the bank holding hands with Adina.

She gapes at Cashmere trying to figure him out. His pants weren't down to his ankles. His skin glowed as if he'd just gotten done doing a Palmer's commercial. As he walks up behind the woman, and her lady friend, he turns to Adina for a kiss. She returned the affection putting her arm around Cashmere's waist, the way a queen would her king. All eyes were on them at the same time.

"You're so gorgeous." Cashmere compliments her, swinging his hat around backwards. "I'm a lucky ass nigga."

He grinned. "No cap." He leaned toward Adina, whispering in her ear, the warmth of his peppermint breath tickles her skin. Almost all the hairs on her back tingles down her spine. It was all but evident, Cashmere said something she liked. The smile on her face gave her away. After all the shit that white woman talked, she smiles, twirling the ends of her hair between her fingers.

"Oh my." Her Southern accent is as heavy as yesterday. "I wished to God my husband would talk to me like that." Her dimples vanish. "He hasn't looked at me that way in over two and a half years."

"Are you serious right now Deborah." Her girlfriend barks. "A minute ago--" she flung her hand into thin air, "You said black people were a bunch of heathens."

Adina laid eyes on both Deborah, and her friend. "Maybe that's why your husband stopped finding you attractive." Her voice is calm. "You're a racist. And it shows." She grabbed Cashmere's hand. "Come on babe. I think the lady is ready for us." She sarcastically says, rolling her eyes.

(Indistinct chatter between Deborah, and her friend)

"I can help the next one in line please." The teller grinned as she typed information into her computer. "How are y'all doing today?" She hadn't quite looked away from her computer screen yet.
  When she did, Cashmere got her eye first.
  "Are we withdrawing funds, or making a deposit?" She blushed.

Cashmere dug in his pants pocket for the check his grandmother gave to him. He passed it along to the teller, an attractive white woman with hazel eyes. She couldn't have been no older than thirty, or thirty one. Casually dressed in her smart attire, but not overdoing it, a pair of black jeans hugged her slim frame. Her blazer fit tightly over her breasts, a yellow beaded necklace draped around her neck matching her cheery smile. Her long black hair pinned to the right of the back of her head. Her curls spiraling down past her shoulders. She preyed on Cashmere as she glanced over the check. Finally, she asks him for an I.d in order to make the deposit. Cashmere hadn't thought of that part. He pulls out his cellphone to call his grandmother. After five straight rings, he hung up.
  "Maybe she went back to bed babe."
  "Nah."
  Cashmere disagreed. "It's after four o'clock. Around this time, she's up drinking tea and shit." The teller went ahead to open the account. She gulped, almost choking on her spit. Her brain froze. Her eyes count more numbers than she expected them to see.

"Something wrong?" Adina asked.

She moved up against the glass to see the computer screen, but was unable to tell why the banker had such a blind look on her face. She blatantly ignored Adina's question.

"This is a lot of money." Said, the teller.

"Yes."

Adina stepped up. "It is." She sneered at the woman, who obviously came off as a disrespectful ass bitch, that wanted her ass beat. "We want to deposit the check please."   Now Adina is talking a little more aggressively. "Please and thank you." She says, resting her arm on the ledge.

Cashmere loved Adina's attitude. The teller is looking at him as if he would put Adina in her place. Whether Cashmere said anything or not, Adina wasn't letting that happen no way. Nor was she feelin the way the teller was flirting with Cashmere as if she weren't standing right beside him.

"I see four accounts here." The banker says, with an attitude, clearing her throat. "Which account are we using?" She then proceeds to cross her hands.

"Whatchu mean four?" Cashmere quizzed.

His grandmother hadn't mentioned a word to him about either of the accounts. He really included no idea of her funds, or where the money came from. "Baby girl." He shook his hand no. "I don't know what's going on. My NaNa sent me to deposit this check. That's what I'm doing."

"Can you tell us the names on the account?" Adina inquired. "I'm sorry. We've never done this before. We're just trying to help his grandma out. She's sick."

The teller rolls her eyes. Everyone in line could see she was slightly worried, and more annoyed than she was five minutes ago. She stated the names in a low tone. Cashmere being the first one to come out of her mouth. Then she says, "I see Marco Malone. There's Damon Finley, and Ramario Finley."

Cashmere's face turned from placid to appalled. He shouts. "Finley?" His dismayed attitude hit the roof. "I'll tell you what," he says in a more chill manner. "Put half in my account. Whatever is left out, put it in the Marco account." While the teller distributed the funds into both accounts, Cashmere attempted to call his grandmother once again. His heart began to race. Because this is the second time he failed at getting a hold of her.

EXT: 5pm

Fast on his feet, Cashmere hit the alleyway to Kedzie Avenue, Adina hot on his heels. As they're walking on the roughness of the cobbled ground, the sour relics of dumpster juice cause Adina to gag. The smell of old takeout food drowned her eyes in tears. With the back of her right hand, she covers her mouth to cease vomiting. Cashmere stops abruptly, gripping her by the wrist while he calls his grandmother for the fourth time. Her phone went straight to voicemail. Cashmere began to feel as if he couldn't breathe. He's thinking of all the reasons why his grandmother wasn't answering the phone. Anxiety set in, Cashmere paced the filthy cracks in the cement.

"She's not picking up the goddamn phone Adina." Cashmere picks up a beer bottle covered in dust particles, he throws it against the brick wall.

    (Glass shattering)

Adina flinched at the sound of the glass breaking. She felt it in her aura that something bad happened to Elliana, but she wanted to keep Cashmere in one piece until he knew for sure what was going on. Otherwise he was bound to go crazy.

"Babe."

Adina pulled him close to her. "Woosah." She whispers.

Her fingers are gentle on his lips as she succeeded in temporarily, quieting him down. Once he got his cool back, he hit Marco up on the speed dial. He needed to blow some serious steam. And Marco was definitely with the shits. The thought of Finley's name brought anger to Cashmere's head. He visualized himself kidnapping Finley, putting a bullet in his skull. Marco hadn't answered the phone yet. While Cashmere's wearing a groove in the ground, calling Marco back to back, the leaning of the apartment buildings distract Adina. She's staring up at the broken windows, and rusted air conditioners. Each of the buildings were so close together, it felt as though they were caving in on her. She crossed her arms over her chest.

(Tires Screeching)

Out of nowhere, a black Suburban truck with tinted windows came burning dust up the alleyway toward Cashmere and Adina. The driver damn near ran into the dumpster as it swerved, almost tipping over. Cashmere thought to himself, he should have taken the main street on Kedzie, but chose to take the quick route. Realizing the person driving wasn't stopping, Cashmere squeezed Adina's hand. They took off running through puddles of stale water. Adina gapes back over her shoulder. She became nervous.

"Babe who's that?" She pants. "Why are they chasing us?" She's holding her hand across her breasts as Cashmere keeps her close to him. "What do they want from us?" She's asking, glaring back and forth over her shoulder.

Cashmere drew his weapon from the waistline of his jeans aiming straight at the windshield. Both the driver, and passenger duck.

(Gunshots)
(Glass shattering)
(Lights flashing)

Cashmere guards Adina behind him, shielding her with his life. Unbeknownst to him, Adina never went outside without protection of her own. Beneath her tongue, she kept a razor in case she needed to draw a permanent smile on someone's face. She guards Cashmere's backside. Her hands on his hips. Her eyes are glued to the vehicle that has them trapped against a red brick wall.
(Heavy Breathing)

The door opened. Cashmere got into full murder mode. He pulled the trigger, busting out the front headlight. Adina squeezed him tight as she kissed the back of his head. She easily spit the razor out of her mouth. Relieved to see a familiar face, Cashmere tranquilized himself. Big Lo rolled up. Marco jumps out of Big Lo's whip. He's higher than a damn air force one. Cashmere raised an eyebrow. The beating in his chest hadn't slowed down just yet.

"Nigga where the fuck you been?" He howls. "I called you three times."

"Nigga I was looking for yo ass." Marco responded, his words slurred. Cashmere tucks his pistol back in his pants.

"I gotta get home bruh. I think something is wrong with NaNa."

"Bruh," says, Marco. "Shit got real. I just left the crib. It's all fucked up." He explains, gritting his teeth. "NaNa wasn't in the crib-- He lights a half of a blunt-- "At all my nigga."

He inhaled the weed, exhaling a cloud grey of smoke. Cashmere encouraged Adina to go home while he went to check on his grandmother.

"I'll call you later." He said, kissing her on the lips. That was the last thing Adina wanted to hear. She raised her voice, taking control the same way she's been doing. "Go home?" She spat. "Boy I'm not leaving you."

Marco stood to the side. He inhaled the longest drag into his lungs.
(Coughing)

"Better get her lil pretty ass a burner bruh." His eyes are bloodshot red. He's giggling. "On the lowski, her ass is crazy, crazy."

CONTIN....

Bulldozers submerged Fuller Park in debris. Broken glass everywhere. Chipped pieces of taillights lay in the street. Holes, the size of basketballs imprinted in car windows. The City of Chicago annihilated everybody's home on the block. Cashmere rolled his window down, the cold wind stinging his lips. He snarled at the sight of his block shredded to pieces.

"Aye Big let me out."

"Babe." Adina stopped him. "The street is blocked off."

"I don't--" Cashmere growls, "Give a fuck right now." He pounds his fist into the palm of his hand. "I'm going in the crib." He sneered. "And so help me God--" The anger in Cashmere's eyes turned to fire. His voice seemed deeper, and sexier than the first time Adina met him. She visualized him going buck wild, stomping somebody's face in.

"If my NaNa ain't in there when I walk through that door--" The uncomfortable noise of Cashmere's teeth grind on each other. "I'm lighting shit the fuck up." He gawks at Adina. "Period pooh."

(Gun Cocks)

"Bae."
Adina smirks.
"What Adina."
Cashmere replied, gazing out of the window at the snowflakes that began falling to the ground.

Adina slid closer to him. Her whispers were the sweetest thing next to strawberry lemonade.
Cashmere stares at her with that bad boy, menacing look on his face. He's leaned back his thumb and index finger in the shape of an L underneath his chin. The print in his pants has eyes of their own. Adina bit her bottom lip. She held Cashmere close to her until they pulled up to his grandmother's house.

INT. Evening- 5:15pm- Elliana Jeans House

Cashmere used the back door, leading to the kitchen to enter his house. Papers were scattered on the floor, the lamp shades were tilted over, pictures of his grandparents, torn to pieces. The sofa wasn't a sofa anymore. Instead, it'd been clawed as if Freddy himself sliced it in half. Cashmere's skin became inflamed with cold chills. His temperature hit the roof. He was damn near hyperventilating as he walked through the house(Glass cracking) calling his grandmother's name. Adina gasped.

"I know you don't want to hear this babe." She utters over his shoulder. No amount of words could be said for Cashmere to believe, someone would kidnap the woman who raised him his entire life. The kiss of Adina's soft lips were pressed against Cashmere's collarbone.

"I honestly don't think your grandma is here."

The whisper of Adina's voice brought Cashmere to his knees. He's in a disoriented state, not realizing his head went low. Sousing in harsh truth, Adina made sure to squeeze Cashmere from behind. Enough for him to feel safe in her arms, and shed a few tears, and he did. It wasn't easy for her to witness Cashmere as a jovial being. Then turn around to see him angry, confused, and hurt by night. His brokenness took her to a different level of wanting to console him. Her actions portrayed her to be loyal no matter the situation.

(Cashmere sniffling)

"We'll find her babe." Adina muttered. She knew as well as Cashmere did, her words slid into his mind. "I promise." Her hands went from touching his chin hairs. "Okay." She entwined their fingers. "I'm not going anywhere." She assured. "Ever." Cashmere didn't expect Adina to be so compassionate, but he knew at that moment, she wanted him for life as much as he wanted to love her forever, beyond words.

CONTIN....

Cashmere went to his grandmother's bedroom to investigate. He planned on finding anything that would tell him what connections her and Finley had together. Instantly, Cashmere recorded the photos he'd seen before. He got to digging through his grandmother's dresser drawers until he located a separate photo album. (Whew) He blew the dust off of it. As he skims over the photos, he sees pictures of Finley, and his grandmother. That didn't strike a nerve no more than seeing another familiar face in the next photo. It was Paco. Cashmere slammed the book shut, lunging it across the room. Perplexed to know his grandmother dealt with Finley, ignited his snafu.

EXT. Outside

"I want him fucking dead my nigga." Cashmere blurted out to Marco.
"My boy--" Marco inquired. "You gotta be more specific."
"That nigga Finley." Cashmere growled. "I want him--" He angrily bit his lips, "Dead, buried in the dirt"
Adina jumped in as a tranquilizer. She thought it might be a good idea for them to go grab a bite to eat, and give Cashmere time to clear his head.

Chapter 10

INT: West Lake Street- L Train-The Robbery

Adina, Marco, and Cashmere jogged down the beat up steps to catch the L train on West Lake Street. They walked side by side underground til they reached the self automated machine to purchase their train tickets. Stale air clogged their noses as they got toward the last step. Graffiti on the walls were drawn to their eyes. As they head through the metal detector, a rush of gross wind blows over their heads. The only thing occupying the cracks in the platform is their boots and sneakers. Beneath the dim lights, there's nothing but a black tunnel ahead of them. It almost looked like a crime scene.

   A man who, identified as part of the Italian mafia, gapes at Adina from across the train tracks. He's dressed in a beige suit. His thick mustache is spread above his lip. The darkness in his chocolate brown eyes gave Adina chills. He sat there on the bench, his leg fancied over his left thigh reading a newspaper. Gold rings glitter off of his ring, and pinky fingers. The hair is visible on his chest showing off his golden cross necklace.

   He gawked at Cashmere one time before laying the paper down beside him. Adina kept her eyes away from him. She stayed on Cashmere's hip, holding his hand until they sat down.

(Indistinct chatter)

   "Keep your eyes on the briefcase." Said the cop standing next to him.

The Italian man whose name is Enrico Russo rose to his feet. "Uffa." He says, bored of the cop and his bossy antics. His smile is as fierce as it is handsome.

   "Stronzo." Russo spoke in a nonchalant way, calling the cop an asshole. "Just make sure the deal goes through." He says, glaring over his shoulder.

Russo almost cracked a smile, when he felt something nibbling at his ankle. A filthy Norway rat with brown fuzz on its back is biting at his pants leg, claiming its territory. The rat became hostage to Russo's bare hands. He laughs, holding the creature by its neck up to the cops face. The cop began feeling sick to his stomach. He's looking at the oversized furry rodent. Russo choked the rat to death til its eyes bulged out of its sockets, and cries came to be quiet. The cop spit up on himself.

Russo let the corpse of the rodent fall to the cement, not a bit of sorrow on his honeycomb complexioned face. He pulls a wet wipe from the inside of his jacket pocket to clean his hands. Disgusted, the cop is overly anxious for his lieutenant to show up with the money for the kilos of cocaine. He's wiping the saliva from his mouth,
(Italian Mafia Music Playing) when he sees the lieutenant coming down the steps in his kangaroo, brown leather shoes.

(Italian Mafia Music Playing)
Two Smith, and Wesson pieces are fully loaded in Russo's holster, just in case the lieutenant and his protege wanted to go to war.

CONTIN...

Across the tracks, Cashmere and Marco peep funny activity between Russo and the police officer. Their intuition tells them something is getting ready to go down. Cashmere subtly whispers in Adina's ear. "Tie your sneakers up tight. Stay close to me." Marco kept an unenthusiastic posture. In a matter of seconds, their lives were going to change.

Russo stood to his feet. A man in a fedora hat, who happened to be the lieutenant approached him. He's suited in purple. A trench coat tailored to his mid-knee. His footsteps, the only sound on the pavement of the subway. But there's a weary death note in the air. He's carrying a briefcase in his left hand. He smiles at his officer. In return, he got a devious grin back. The men greet one another.

"Mr. Russo."

"Buonasera lieutenant."

The men shake hands. However, their body language didn't match the friendly, business smiles on their faces. The lieutenant played it off as if he were passing the briefcase to Russo. His eyes are still. The dimples in his cheeks sneak rise. His posture is subtle, but windy.
(Italian Mafia Music Playing)
Instead of giving the money to Russo, he tossed it into the hands of the cop. He clutched the briefcase against his chest. He jumps off of the platform. He's running alongside the tracks. The lieutenant retrieved his weapon the same time as Russo. (Italian Mafia Music Playing) Screeching sounds from the train takeover the atmosphere. Gunshots are being fired as the train is coming down the tracks. Russo popped the lieutenant at point blank range. Also taking a hit to his abdomen. The noise of the gunshots brought Cashmere back to that night, where he just about died in front of the mini market. It felt as if the bullet was still in his guts. There's a lurching feeling in his stomach. Every gunshot tore Cashmere from reality. The men pulling the triggers definitely felt warm blood gushing out of them.

Cashmere had no recollection of the present until Adina grabbed his hand. She squeezed him close to her. The train is getting closer to the platform. Winds are coming in at ten miles per hour, blowing dust everywhere.

"You ready?"

Cashmere utters.

Adina stares at him, then nods at her sneakers. They're laced up, just like Cashmere said. He gave her a fast kiss on the lips. The train is closer than it had been a few minutes ago. Time is running out. They leap onto the rusted tracks, over to the other side of the platform. Cashmere knelt down as a ladder to lift Adina up on his shoulders. She crawled on top of the ledge of the platform. She reached her hand back down to help Cashmere to his feet. He grabbed her hand using all his strength to get himself up on the ground. Once they were able to stand up, they walked over to Russo.

Cashmere checked his pulse. Russo was losing consciousness.

"Adina get the briefcase."

"Okay." She says, out of breath, picking the bag up. "Got it."

Blood began to ooze from the corner of Russo's mouth, staining the already dirty pavement. His gorgeous skin is now discolored in a fountain of blood. He raised his weak arm, clenching onto Cashmere's shirt. He's fighting the fatality of his departure. "Get-- he wheezed, choking on his own blood. His veins are bulging out of his neck. "The co--" Russo didn't have to say another word before he died. Cashmere knew what was being asked of him. He retrieved Russo's pistol, admiring the gold trim. He walked toward the lieutenant. His breathing is rattled as he applies pressure to his wound. Cashmere pressed the pistol against the lieutenant's temple. The remaining bullet for death. And not a chance to miss.

"Crooked cops don't last long in Chicago."
 Cashmere put the lieutenants lights out. His eyes cracked into a look that became normal more and more everyday. That look of no return.

EXT. Train Tracks- The Chase- Escaping

The only thing left to do was find Marco. Cashmere didn't want to be pessimistic, but he couldn't see a damn thing. Nor could he hear anything beyond the footsteps of the many people getting off of the train.
(People screaming)
Train riders got a glimpse of the two dead men lying on the pavement. They scattered like mice, running toward the steps. Some of them even stayed on the train as a way to protect themselves. Meanwhile Cashmere, and Adina crept along the wall of the tracks. The further they go, the darker the tunnel gets. For the first time, Adina was scared. The blackness of the tunnel blurred her vision of seeing Cashmere, but she felt him holding onto her. They're walking hip to hip when Cashmere tripped over a lump of something hard. Instantly, he got sick to his stomach. Using his better judgement, Cashmere placed his hands on what caused him to fall flat on his face. The material on his hands is rough. He kept on feeling around until he felt the aluminum police officers badge. Cashmere sighed, relieved it wasn't Marco's body.   "We gotta find my brother." He jumped to his feet, swallowing the spit in his mouth.
 "Marco." He yelped. "Where you at, bruh?"
Cashmere began to panic at the silence in the tunnel. His very own eyes were scaring him. Everything is pitch black. Adina cut her flashlight on, shining it toward the end of the tunnel. There was Marco slithering on his side in a pond of

blood. He groaned with every breath he took. Cashmere's legs grew fragile as he sped off racing down the metal train tracks. He's breathing, but the air didn't feel like it was going into his lungs. Instead, it felt as if he were jogging under water. His feet were moving, but his upper body felt heavier than what it really was. When he finally got to Marco's side, he felt dizzy like he wanted to pass out. He sprawled toward Marco on his hands, scraping his knees on dirty ol' used heroin syringes.

Marco hadn't realized, the cop stabbed him in the torso. His adrenaline was so high, the only thing he knew was getting the briefcase full of money. Cashmere propped Marco up in his arms.

The fear of losing him, dressed his face like a pillow over his mouth and nose. Marco was slowly keeping himself alive. But somehow, he couldn't smile. He wished the pain would go away.

"Bruh, I gotchu' Cashmere squeezes Marco close to him. "O--" Marco whispered. "Oka--" He stuttered.

Cashmere gaped at Adina, scowling with nothing to say. Adina's body movements are still. "Just tell me what you want me to do babe." She sniffles, the tears cascade down her cheeks. She doesn't want to leave Cashmere alone. However, there wasn't much of a choice.

"Get the briefcase." Cashmere tells her. "And get out of here. I'll come find you later." His palms are sweating. He's clutching Marco tighter wanting to beat the fuck out of that crooked police officer.

"Cashmere, I can't." Adina whimpered. "You know that." She whined, wiping the tears from her eyes.

Cashmere gently laid Marco down for a split second to embrace Adina. The minute he wrapped her in his arms, her legs lost their feelings. Her arms gripping him tighter, and tighter around his neck. Tear after tear, she cried on Cashmere's shoulder. Conscious of her love for him, he held Adina by the chin. He kissed her in a way that made her feel safe.

"Babe." She dried her eyes. "If I don't hear from you by midnight," She began to cry again, her voice cracks, it's dry. She picks up the briefcase holding it against her thigh. The bit of light shining from her cellphone, allowed her to look Cashmere deep in the eyes. "I am coming to look for you." She says. Cashmere could see the waves in Adina's eyes. Her words are golden. She said what she meant, and meant what she said.

INT. Adina's House- 11:45pm- The Hallway

A headache struck Adina's temple as she laid in bed on her side, waiting to hear Cashmere knock on the door. It reminded her of her mother. So many nights, she saw her mom sitting in a dark room at 2am wondering where her father was. But this was different. Adina wasn't up waiting for a lying ass cheater to come home to her. She was waiting for the love of her life. Everytime the hand on the clock ticked closer to 12, Adina cringed. She climbed out of bed to look through the peephole on the front door. A narrow hallway, and dirty walls is all that's in front of her. She paced the floor, thinking whether or not to go back out and find her man. She raised her arm to move the curtains back. The streets were quiet. There's nothing outside except overflowing trash cans of soda bottles, and leaning stop signs. Adina glared at the time in the microwave. Cashmere has five minutes to show up.

Adina ran to her room, she hid the briefcase far under her bed, where she assumed it wouldn't be found. Afterwards, she grabbed her coat to head out the door. When she got to the steps, her heart sank to the pit of her stomach.

"You're all bloody." She uttered, pulling her coat over her shoulder. She held onto the banister, crossing her arm over her torso.

"Told you I'd find you." Cashmere said, walking up the broken staircase.

His footsteps hardly echoed. Instead they are sluggish, and tired. Blood stains are on his hands.
His clothes are covered in dirt. The one thing that held Adina's attention, is the print in Cashmere's jeans. She stood at the top of the staircase, slinked in the shadows of the dim light. She breathed to get closer to Cashmere. He looked just as fine smudged in dirt. When he finally gets to her, she falls into his arms. In moments of discerning his love for Adina, Cashmere's eyes are perfect for her. More soft than he imagined them to be. Neither one of them stopped gazing at each other. Their lips brush together. It's not an innocent kiss either. It's hot, fiery. Adina couldn't pull back. Her senses were being seduced.

Cashmere has a way of touching her. Each time she felt his hands on her skin, the floor fell from under her feet. She ran her fingers across his stomach, pulling him toward her until there was no air left between them to breathe.

"Pull ya' pants down." Cashmere demands, pinning Adina against the wall, "And pull ya' panties to the side." He kissed her neck.

His voice is deeper than the silence in the entire building. Wiggling out of her jeans, Adina glared over her shoulder at Cashmere's smooth brown face. She held herself up with one hand, moving her bikini cut panties to the side with the other hand. Cashmere's penis began to swell up. He glanced at Adina's round ass. A second later, he found himself gently, thrusting the head of his rod into her vagina.

"Oh my God, bae." Adina moaned, gasping.

She plunged forward, arching her back. Normally, Adina would never physically touch the greasy walls. But all she could feel was Cashmere taking her to cloud nine. He reached around to grab her chin. He met her lips with a five second kiss. Then continued to stroke her moist vagina. His knees are slightly bent. He's using his leg muscles to push upward. With every stroke, Adina moaned Cashmere's name.

"Babe."

She exhaled. "I'm yours."

She bites her lip. "I love you Cashmere."

The words I love you made Cashmere fuck Adina passionately. Pleasure flashed beneath the surface of his face. His eyes fell upon her brown skin down to her lower back. His mouth hung open for the taste of her pussy on his tongue.

As Adina bounced her ass back on Cashmere's rock hard shaft, she wore the expression of being young and in love. Her eyes are simply the candles to Cashmere's heart.

"Fuck baby girl." He groans.

"You make my dick feel good as fuck."

He grabs Adina by the waist, pulling her towards him. Their climax is creeping up on the both of them. A smile is a mile away from their faces. Only intense gazes getting Cashmere closer to his nut. The feeling of him cumming rocked Adina's world upside down. In that present moment, warm goosebumps showed themselves between

her thighs. The wetness of Cashmere exploding inside of her made her fall deeper in love. She oozed cream all over his dick til' it ran down her inner thigh. Cashmere collapsed on Adina's backside.
(Heavy breathing)
He kissed her bare skin, the taste of her melanin is rich. She wiped her finger alongside her sticky thigh, sticking it in Cashmere's mouth. She stared at him with love in her eyes. Afterwards, she pulled her pants up over her wet booty.
(Silence)

INT. Finley Makes A Drug Sale- Finley Interrogates Cashmere

Cashmere is sitting sideways on the stairs. His back against the wall. He's caressing Adina's arms, thinking about Marco. Adina leaned her head backwards, pouting her lips out for a kiss.
Cashmere gazed at her. With everything that's happened, Adina's been the only one by his side.
Not once did she complain or threaten to walk away. She squeezed his arms in hers.
 "Your brother okay?" She uttered in a caring voice.
 "My nigga got nine lives." Cashmere cackled, turning his Yankee hat to the back of his head.
"That's what it seems like."
 (Emotional Piano Music Playing)
His moment of joy quickly vanished. His eyes swelled up with fret. The minute he burst into tears, Adina threw her arms around him. She cuffed him close to her, kissing his forehead. The blood on his clothes is still a fresh memory for them both. Cashmere held Adina tight, appreciating her comforting him.

CONTIN....

(Indistinguishable Chatter)
"Yea." Says, Finley. I'm here."
The urgency in his voice is evident. He came to serve a fiend and get back on the block to monitor Kedzie Avenue. He reached the steps and began to laugh.
"Aren't y'all cute." He sarcastically says, coming up the stairwell.
"I heard cha' boy got stabbed up."
Cashmere sprawled to his feet. Adina clutched him by the arm.
"Babe." She utters.
Cashmere loosened his way out of Adina's grip on him. He and Finley met midway on the staircase. Cashmere growls through clenched teeth.
"My momma wasn't there for me." The smell of his Versace cologne is quite impressive to Finley. He's standing there silent. "My bro is laid up in the hospital, my grandma is missing."   Cashmere retrieved his pistol from his waistline.
"I ain't got much more to lose. Ya dig?"
He shrugged his shoulders, pointing the weapon in Finley's face.
"So if you gone roll up on me and my girl, you better ask the right ma fuckin' questions."   The dim lights gave Cashmere the look of a grim reaper, dressed in blood. His skin is darker. His eyes are less bright. And his demeanor is cold. His finger is on the trigger. He's looking at Finley. Finley is gaping back at him. He burst out giggling.   "I might be able to help you find ya' grandmother."   His cheeks rise into a mysterious smile.
"But you have to do something for me."

"Nigga I ain't ask for ya' help."
Cashmere is so angry, he nearly pushed Finley down the steps. Finley staggered back from the direct blow to his chest.
(Finley Chuckles)
"Fine by me."
He brushed by Cashmere to meet Diana, the junkie at the top of the staircase. He put the product in her hand. In exchange, she paid him the cash. That fast, it was over. Finley grabbed her by the throat. She gasped at how strong he was.
"I better not find out you've been buying from other motha fuckas in my house."
"You won't." Diana swore. "I promise." Saliva dripped from the sides of her mouth. Finley unleashed her. The fright on her face stayed there until he left. The chrome on his badge sparkled in the dark as he jogged down the steps. He grinned at Cashmere making his way out into the cold.

Chapter #11

EXT. One Week Later- Evening- Cashmere Is Looking For His Grandmother

The corner of Kedzie Avenue is where the dirtiest money was made. Every minute of the day, a prostitute is out there tricking. Because of the unsafe activities, neighbors rarely ever came out of their home.
Cashmere sat on the steps of an abandoned house. The charcoal painted door is hanging off its hinges. The porch is old and slippery with rain from last night. Cashmere constantly checked his pager. His grandmother still hadn't contacted him. He sighed, putting the device back in his

pants pocket. Cashmere put his head between his legs, swaying side to side. The anger in his heart came from being away from the one woman he loved the most. His grandmother. Everything made him angry. Gangs, cars, the butt naked women right before his eyes. Truth is, Cashmere was going through a midlife crisis. And it's more than what his brain can handle.

   A woman with long brown legs and thick thighs came treading down the same sidewalk that Cashmere is on. She was dressed, the same as all of the other prostitute junkies. Yet something about her stood out. Her hair is combed back into two french braids. Nothing extravagant, just enough to keep the baby hairs out of her eyes.

   She gets a side glance of Cashmere's chocolate skin. His body language is not all that positive. She pulls a Newport one hundred from her Chanel purse. "You look like you need one of these." She lights the cancer stick. It brought a sweet rush to her fingers.

   Cashmere looks up at her. He accidentally gave her the shitty end of the pole.

   "Girl get the fuck away from me." He spat, paying attention to everything else except her.

   Her head slowly fell off to the side. "That was rude." She replied, turning to walk away. Cashmere had to get a grip on himself. He was completely out of his mind. He quickly hopped up on his feet.

   "My fault shawty." He reached for her arm. "I ain't mean to come at you like that." He lifts his hat up, just to pull it back down. She plucked the ashes to her cigarette on the cement. The smoke flurrying in front of both their eyes.

   "I forgive you." She says, taking another drag. "I'm guessing you don't smoke these." She giggles.

   "Nah."

Cashmere sits back on the steps.
The weather is cold enough that his hands shiver inside of his pockets.
"We should go someplace warm." The prostitute suggests.
Cashmere squints his eyes at a woman he sees standing on the corner of Kedzie Avenue. It wasn't hard to tell, it was his mother. A tacky maroon dress hung off of her body. Her wig needed a nap. Cashmere gawked at her from afar. A disgusting look on his face. He stands to his feet, rubbing his hands against each other to warm them up.
"I'll be right back." He communicated to the prostitute.

Cashmere crossed the street. His mother is so high on Molly, she didn't see him coming her way. She's leaning in the window of a car. Her ankles tremble as the cold breeze hits her skin. Cashmere stands there rigid as the chief of police. His backbone seemed to be as straight as the pole he's leaning on. The street lights shimmer, flickering off and on. Alexis pops her head out of the car window for a brief moment. Her cheeks are sunk in. She's not the same anymore. Every bit of her beauty has been stolen from using drugs.
(Tense Music Playing)
(Indistinct Chatter)
"I'll pay you back this week. I swear."
The drug dealer Alexis was buying from never took anything less than what was owed to him. Forty dollars meant nothing. He wanted the whole hundred. Which Alexis didn't have. He knocked her in the mouth. She stumbled backwards on her ass. Blood gushing from her gums. Afterwards, he sped off down the block.

Alexis helped herself to her feet. She crosses her bony arms over her chest. Her shoes echoe off the concrete. Heavy winds go against her back causing her to walk crooked. The heel of her shoe gets caught in the cracks of the ground. She tripped, skinning her knee on the pavement. *(Emotional Saxophone Music Playing)*

"Alexis."

The rumble in Cashmere's voice swirled around her, carrying her to a place where she remembers being a mother.

(Alexis Crying)

"Go--" she stutters, "Away Cashmere." She wipes the blood from her mouth. "I don't want you seeing me like this."

The sound of Alexis crying was her heart breaking into pieces. Each tear carved streaks on the flesh of her face.

"I know you love me Alexis."

Cashmere tried hiding his grief. "You got to." He shrugged. "I'm your only son." He couldn't do it. He broke down entirely.

"I'm so sorry son."

(Emotional Saxophone Music Playing)

Alexis stares up at her Cashmere. He's pacing around in circles. Red-hot tears fall from his golden brown eyes.

"Get up ma." He attempts to help her up.

Weak in the knees, Cashmere wound up grieving in his mother's arms on the cold sidewalk.

"I love you son." She murmured. "I've always loved you."

(Emotional Saxophone Music Playing)

INT. Nine Days Later- Joe's Seafood Restaurant

With everything that had happened in the last month, Adina thought it'd be a healthy idea for her and Cashmere to get some food in their stomachs. They picked Marco up in an uber from the hospital and headed to Joe's Seafood Restaurant. Adina ordered Joe's Chopped Salad which included tomato, cucumber, carrots, black olives, Honey Roasted Peanuts, and Joe's special vinaigrette dressing. Everything on the salad sounded appealing except the black olives. She smiled asking for extra feta cheese instead of the olives.

"Oh." Adina says. "May I have--"

"May I?"

Marco laughed with a lap full of one hundred dollar bills. "Yo." He looks at Cashmere. "Ya' girl is like God's twin or some shit." He said chuckling.

(Adina giggling)

"Be quiet Marco." She playfully slapped him on the arm. "As I was saying," she rolled her eyes at him.

"May I please have a glass of lemon water?"

The waiter wrote everything on his notepad. Cashmere wasn't all the way there. Adina asked him if he figured out what he wanted to eat. He just shrugged his shoulders. "I'll take the--" she leaned her head to the side real cute. "We'll have the Jumbo Shrimp Cocktail please, and Oysters, thank you."

"Whole or half shell?" Asked the waiter.

"Whole shell." Answers Marco. "And a beer." He jokes.

"For a person who got stabbed and almost died," Adina jokes, "You are so goofy." She shook her head laughing.

"Nah." (Laughing)

Marco lays his gun on the table. The waiter's eyes got big. "Let me get a Coke, no ice, and a Pepsi for my mans."

"Please and thank you," says Adina.

Cashmere babysat his phone by the second, wishing his grandmother returned his phone call. The gloss in his eyes eventually built up tears. He sniffled, a single teardrop cascading down on his cheek. Then another one until he couldn't hold back. Adrenaline sped through his veins. Slouched in his seat, he rubbed his hand across his forehead. The weary look on his face was of someone whose dog died. Raising his arm, he turned his fitted hat around to the back of his head. Fear of his grandmother lying somewhere dead, looped in his thoughts until he could think of nothing else.

  Adina gawked Cashmere in the eyes. The tears in them appeared so rapidly, it was utterly impossible for her to say anything to console him. However, she used her listening spirit to support him. Her love for Cashmere is like a meadow, a quiet place to self reflect. "Babe we can cancel the order--" she entangled her arm into his, peering him in the eye, "And go look for her." She pecked his cheek. "She couldn't have gotten that far on her walker." Cashmere pulled away from her. "I need some space." He says, leaving his phone behind on the table. Adina's eyes swelled up with tears. The waiter just got to their table holding hot plates of food on both his arms.

  "Shrimp Cocktail." He grinned. "And salad."

  "Thank you."

  Adina's sniffling over her food. She'd already lost her appetite. She pushed the salad away from her, tears steady streaming down her cheeks.

  "I'll be back with the oysters." Said the waiter.

  "It's cool man." Marco nodded.

The waiter walked off, Marco hopped in the seat beside Adina. She wanted to hold back her tears, but struggled to do so. Marco's shoulder became a pillow to her cheeks. He kept it gangsta with her as she hid, crying in the palm of her hand. Nobody knew Cashmere the way Marco did. He wiped Adina's eyes with his trigger finger.

"Give him some time to cool off aiight." He muttered. "His ass ain't going nowhere." (Cashmere's Phone Ringing)

Marco couldn't answer the phone fast enough. A wind of relief swept over him, when NaNa's name flashed across the screen. He swiped the green call button to answer the phone. There was a different voice on the other end, a stern male's tone with a heavy Italian accent. Marco made a scene in the restaurant, startling everyone from enjoying their food. He hollered into the phone.

"Who the fuck is this on my NaNa's phone?"
(Man laughing)

"Yea pussy." Marco yelped. "You won't be laughing when I find you." He cocked his gun-- "And put a bullet in ya ma fucking mouth homie."

Everyone in the restaurant began screaming. They grabbed their children, dashing for cover beneath the table. Some of them ran straight out of the door. The manager approached Marco, asking him to put his pistol down. They got into a scuffle. Marco sucker punched the manager so hard, he fell backwards over a chair. Trying to grab hold of something as he went tumbling, the manager pulled the tablecloth down, spilling drinks on his face and lips. By that time, Adina came flying through the door with Cashmere on her tail feather.

"Bruh wassup?" He inquired about his grandmother. "Adina said, you were on the phone with
NaNa." He says, reaching for his pistol in the back of his pants. "Where the fuck is she at?"   "Bruh I don't know

where she is." Marco emphasized the bass in his voice. "Some clown ass nigga called me from her phone laughing and shit."

Adrenaline raced through Cashmere's body to the point, he blacked out as he, Adina and Marco were leaving the restaurant. The last thing Cashmere had recollection of was Finley and his partner, Williams' face. The inside of the restaurant seemed to have spun around twelve times. Adina's screaming for Cashmere to stop. Her eyes began to swell as the tears came rolling down her cheeks.
　"You're gonna go to jail." She wept out loud, babe stop.
　Finley threw body shots at Cashmere, hitting him in the rib. Adina wasn't taking another round of Finley putting his hands on her man. She spit out her razor, slashing Finley across the back of his neck.
　"Aahh, SHIT." He howled. Blood trickled down his spine. He wiped the back of his neck with his hand. "Imma' let that slide. Because you're a female."
Cashmere rolled over on his side in excruciating pain. He retrieved his pistol, groaning.　"I'll see your lil dumb ass around." Finley cracked up laughing.

EXT. Kedzie Avenue- Early Morning

Walking the streets of Kedzie Avenue after dark was like a blur. The paint on the apartment buildings is chipped. Most of the windows hadn't been replaced in years. The banisters, like all of the other ones were leaning, and unsteady. Whatever color they used to be had faded away. It's as cold as ice outside. High winds shook off the last of the leaves, lighting up the sidewalk a red and orange color. Each of Adina, Cashmere, and Marco's footsteps made a

crunch sound everytime they stepped on a leaf. Thin branches were all that they saw on the trees still standing. Adina shivers, taking her house keys out of her jacket pocket. By the time they reached her apartment, it was completely night time. She scurried up the cracked steps.
   Cashmere and Marco's sneakers thudding against them as they follow her up to the door to go inside. The dim porch light didn't make it easy for Adina to unlock the door. The steel knob froze her hand as she twisted it to her left.

INT. The Hallway- Adina Helps A Homeless Man

Inside of the gloomy building, it's cold and dreary. A homeless man is lying on the floor sleeping.
He barely looked like he was breathing.
   Adina abruptly stopped, staring at him, swallowing the spit in her mouth. Her heart began to race, thinking about her own well-being. Cashmere dug in his pocket for some cash. He gives Adina a twenty dollar bill.
   "Go head." He says. "I know you want to."
Her footsteps have a quiet sound; someone who doesn't want to be heard. Each of her steps are spaced apart. She kneels down to put the money in a safe place. Suddenly the man popped his eyes open. He is just as scared as Adina. He's cussing, pulling at her coat. Tears roll over his ashy cheeks. "You tryna' rob me?" He says. "I ain't got shit." He's slobbering on himself. "I ain't got SHIT." He yells, slurring his words.
   "My man." Cashmere pats his shoulder. "It's aiight."   He gawks the intimidated man in the eyes.

"My girl just wanted to put a couple dollars in ya' pocket." The man got control of himself. One look at Adina's gorgeous eyes, he fell back against the wall. Dressed in one layer of clothing, he shivered everytime the wind blew through the cracks of the wood door. His flesh stunk up the area. There is little to no life in his face. He may as well have been dead alive. Adina felt joy seeing Cashmere be vulnerable with the homeless man. He hadn't been much of a nice person during the last two weeks. Things were still rocky. And they would be until he found his grandmother safe and sound.

INT. Adina's House- Adina's Mom Comes Home

The apartment hadn't changed much since the last time Adina was there. From the narrow hallway to the living room, Adina frowned. Her eyes wandered over the empty space. Her mother was absent. Her father most likely was ripping and running the streets. Wherever either of them were, Adina missed her mother the most. She investigated their tiny apartment. Her mother's clothes were still in the dresser drawers. So was her fathers belongings. There was a basket of clean laundry in the middle of the living room floor. Adina glanced at, but didn't touch it. Cranberry juice was the only sign of anything to drink. It was left on the counter top unopened.

"I guess we can go to my room," says Adina. Her voice is low. Her eyes were filled with sadness and sleep. Cashmere grabbed her around the waist. He kissed her cheek, squeezing her close to him.

"You want a house babe?" He whispered loudly. "I'll buy you a house." He nibbled on her earlobe. "I'll do whatever you want me to." He turned her towards him. Her eyes

were already wet. Cashmere wiped her eyelids with his thumb.
(Indistinct Chatter In The Hallway)

"We gotta be fast." Avah says, to Jianna. "My husband comes home*(Door Opens)*and finds me packing my things to leave him, I'm dead."

Avah's first glimpse is her daughter. She quickly cleaned the cocaine from under her nose. Her skin didn't look unclean, but her wig was a little crooked. It looked as if she'd been on the block, selling her ass all night. Her and Jianna both wreaked of dick and cum. Their perfume wore off, the after smell afterwards was dingy. Avah walked toward her daughter high as a fan.

"I need to talk to you."

Every other second, she clawed at her nose, scratching the skin off of her ears. Adina stood in silence waiting for her mother to say whatever she had to say. When she stopped scratching, she put her hand on her hip.

"I have to get away from your father." She silently blurted out.

"I'm going to Cali with my new best friend."

She cracks a smile, staring back at Jianna. Adina gives Jianna the look of death. She looks back at her mother with an unhappy face.

"Okay." She says, walking toward her bedroom.
(Door Slams)
(Avah Crying)

"Are you happy now?"

Cashmere quizzed her. His eyes have no soul in them. His respect for Avah is gone. No words came to mind while standing in front of her. Avah wiped the snot from her nose.

"Promise me you'll take care of my baby girl." She begged.

She left wearing only the clothes on her back and the laundry basket full of a few of her clean outfits.
(Front Door Closes)
Marco stayed out in the living room breaking up his weed, so he could roll up and get lit. He felt Adina's pain of not having a mother around. He knew just what she was going through.

CONTIN....

Cashmere promised Adina he'd never let anything happen to her. He opened the door to her bedroom only to find her in a ball of tears lying under the covers. He kicked his sneakers off and crawled in bed with her. He embraced her until she felt safe. During that moment of being in his arms, Adina faced him. She snuggled her nose deep into the nape of his neck. Her body melted away. Although the heavy feeling of weights in her stomach weighed her down. Her body fluttered at the sound of Cashmere's heart beating against hers. She sunk further into feeling protected and loved by him. Somehow his magic touch made everything smoother.

Chapter #12

EXT. Alexis and Quinn- Mid-Day- 1:30pm

The street life stripped Alexis of her once gorgeous brown face.Drug addiction is her way of making money, looking for that same high she experienced a few weeks ago. Alexis hadn't made a good decision since the day she came home from prison. She allowed Quin to pimp her out on Kedzie Avenue. The more she sold her pussy for money, the more she craved to be loved. She quietly, cried out for help. Unfortunately no one was there to pick her up and put her back together. The last time her son saw her, she was just about dead. Her fashionable taste in clothes looked as though she'd been shopping at the thrift store. It was only a matter of time before she'd end up dead from overdosing on cocaine or beaten to death by Quin.

INT. Adina's Room- Cashmere Consoles Adina

Lucid dreams of her mother leaving last night lingered in her head the minute she opened her eyes. Arising to a cloudy day, Adina listened to the winds blowing against her building. She's feeling sad. Her feet are not ready to hit the floor. She rubs her damp eyes with the inside of her palms. Suddenly, she feels Cashmere's touch on her cheek. His hand moves along to her panties. His lips pressed against the skin of her earlobe.

   Cashmere took the pussy without asking. But he did it in a way that made Adina want to give it to him. She squeezed her pillow tight as Cashmere thrusted himself inside of her. Neither of them are sexually experienced. Their connection to one another is so deep, their bodies automatically gave into each other. Cashmere silently growled in Adina's ear as he pumped on her guts.(*Heavy Breathing*)   Cashmere slid his hand underneath Adina's shirt. He cups her breasts in his hand, kissing her on the lips.

EXT. Alexis and Quin

Alexis and Quin were walking to the Windy City Mini Mart. Quin sold her for money every chance he got. She brought in chump change most of the time. No pimp wanted to spend their money on a washed up female jailbird. She and Quin get to the Windy City Mini Market to pick up a pack of blunts and condoms. They're arguing in an isle full of maxi pads. "You know I can't use Trojan Quin." Alexis argued with him for the fifth time. "Them thangs dry my pussy out too fast." Quin shrugged his shoulders.

"Sounds like a personal problem." He says, slapping her upside the head. "Grab that box of three." He laughed. "Yo' raggedy ass gone be doing a lot of fucking tonight."

Alexis sighed. Instead, she stirred clear of him, walking in the direction of the vitamins. Quin is famous for making a scene.
"That's what you think." She spat, treading ahead of him. The sarcasm in her tone raised the hairs on Quin's eyebrows.

CONTIN...

The cabinets were filled with everything except real food. There was Adobo, spaghetti sauce and no noodles. Raisin Bran Crunch cereal, no milk. Adina looked around the kitchen. Her stomach growled at the thought of finding something good to eat. But there wasn't anything she wanted. Fatigue showed on her face. She remembered her mother keeping a money jar in her bedroom down at the bottom of the closet. She prayed it was still there. She hurried toward her mother's room, praying the jar hadn't disappeared. When she opened the door to her mother's empty space, it felt as if she'd been hit with a brick. The silence was as quiet as a mouse on its feet. Darkness stared back at her.

For a hot minute, Adina stood in the doorway, grasping the doorknob. A lightswitch alongside the wall brightened up the lonely room. Adina checked over to her shoulder. She dead stared the closet as if she was committing a crime. Albeit, the door is steps away from her, she felt far from it, like a witch was crawling up her back.
(Dramatic Music Playing)

Adina reached for the chrome handle. It made a "tsk" sound. She pulled the door toward her until she could see everything. Everything her mother owned hung from iron hangers. Adina knew for sure, her mother would be back for the rest of her belongings. Snapping back to the plan, Adina checked the corners of the closet floor first. There was nothing. Her heart began to race. All she needed was twenty dollars to get breakfast from the Windy City Mini Mart. She stood to her feet to leave the room. And on her way out, something told her to look on the top shelf.

   Standing at 5'3 inches, Adina could barely reach the shelf. She dragged the nightstand over to the closet. She climbed on top of it. A blue round gourmet cookie can caught her eye. It's the kind you could find at your grandmother's house on the counter. Adina grabbed the can. She popped the lid on it. Three crispy, twenty dollar bills were laying there with a bunch of quarters. Just when she was folding the money to put in her pocket, Cashmere chuckles to himself in the doorway.

   "You could have asked me for twenty dollars." He says, seriously. Adina steps down off of the nightstand.

   "Yea, well--" she pushed it back in its spot. "I don't feel comfortable asking no man for money so," she shrugged her shoulders. "My mom used to ask my dad for money. Whenever she did that, he would hit her."

Cashmere walked up to Adina, he laid his hands out for her to see.
"I'm not cha' pops baby girl."
"And I'm not my mother." Adina retorted in a whisper like tone.

EXT. Cashmere and Adina Go To Windy City Mini Mart

(Ding)

The bell on the door is the signature to letting the owner, Rafael know when someone is coming in or going out. He came up to the register holding a trash bag. As handsome as he wanted to be, his thin mustache is neatly trimmed above his upper lip. The scarf tied around his head gave him a tender, masculine look. Born and raised in Chicago, Rafael took over the store at the age of seventeen when his father died. He got to see all the kids on the block grow up into young adults. He saw Adina's face and smiled. He'd been knowing her and Cashmere both ever since they were kids. "Hi Rafael." Adina hugged him.
   "Look at you baby girl." He grinned, playfully pinching her cheek. "Ay." He sighed, pulling the garbage from the trash can. "You're all grown up now." He twirled the bag in a knot, sitting it on the floor.
   Rafael laid eyes on Cashmere as he's placing a clean scented bag inside of the can. "How's that bullet wound son?" He looks up at Cashmere.
   "I'm better." Cashmere answered.
   "I find that hard to believe, my friend." Rafael says, closing the lid to the trash can. "How's your abuelita?" He chuckles. "Ol' Mrs. Elliana Jean. Whew she is a fiesty thing isn't she." Rafael laughed.
   Cashmere shrugged.

"Haven't seen her." His voice cracked. "I'm lookin' for her."

"If I hear anything," Rafael sighed. "I'll be the first to let you know."

CONTIN...
(Indistinct chatter)
Soon after Cashmere and Adina spoke to Rafael, a set of voices rose above the silence.

"Get cho' ass up to that counter and pay for them condoms Alexis."

Quinn shouts, pushing her toward the cash register. The glare in his eyes is dull and hateful. Alexis burst out laughing to save herself from crying. Rage consumed her belly. She felt the heat rising in her ears. She and Quinn battled each other like hungry wolves. He sneered at her, giggling, adding more fuel to the fire. "You think I'm a joke." He snapped.

"Whatever nigga." Alexis ignored him, sucking her teeth.

Her face turned plum red, when she saw Cashmere's face. Quinn is just as surprised. His eyes grew dark and cruel.

"You let this clown ass nigga disrespect you like that."

As clear as Alexis could speak. She said, "I'm doing what I gotta' do to survive." She sniffles, scratching her nose. "Ya' grandmother home." Cashmere sucks his teeth. "Why you wanna' know fo'?"

CONTIN...

Adina didn't want to believe her eyes. Seeing her father with another woman, not her mother was tearing her apart. He drank out of a cheap beer can. His breath reeked of alcohol. Needless to say, he looked like a pimp, dressed in

a taupe colored turtleneck and skinny jeans. The Target watch on his wrist glistened. Overwhelmed in her own head, Adina turned to Cashmere, her voice almost gone. "I'm going home." She said.
 "Where's your mother."
 The act of kindness in Quinn's voice came at a bare minimum.
 "She left."
 Adina roared through tears and clenched teeth. "She left because of you dad." Her voice faded away. Her eyes hung low, tears soaking her eyelids. Rafael came walking toward them. One look at Adina's face, it was clear they were arguing.
 "Everything okay mami?" Rafael aaked. The palm of Adina's hand became her tissue.
Because the tears wouldn't stop falling.
 "My dad is an asshole." Adina spat, racing out of the store.

EXT. 2pm

Cashmere didn't have to think twice. He ran after Adina, grasping her from behind. Cold winds smacked their faces, freezing their hands. Adina is so upset.
 "I freakin' hate him babe." She screamed. "Why is he with her." She yelped, tears of anger sliding down her cheeks. Although Cashmere and his mother didn't have the perfect mother, son relationship, Adina's words stung him like a bee. His arms fell from around her waist.
 "You gone disrespect my momma like that?"
 Adina crossed her arms over her chest. The silence in her body language is still. Her eyes are flooding, but the tears haven't fallen from them yet. Cashmere nodded in a disappointing manner. He uttered, not one word. He just

walked off in the opposite direction. Adina's heart nearly came up out of her throat. Tear drops, the size of grape tomatoes strolled down her cheeks as she watched Cashmere leave and not look back at her.

Chapter #13

EXT. 10:50am- Kedzie Avenue

Cashmere sat on the steps of that same dirty, abandoned house. All sorts of wild thoughts crossed his mind. He missed his grandmother and wished that he could hear her voice. The warm weather relieved him to an extent. He looked side to side. There wasn't much happening on the block. Needless to say, the pimps and hoes we're sure to be out by the time the sun went down.
   A cream colored Bentley comes riding up the street. Music is blaring out of the speakers.
(Daysulan Music Playing)
Hit em up
Hit em up
   The person driving the Bentley parallel parked like a professional ball player.

(Music Playing)
I

g
o
t

t
h
e

gwop, I make a movie I'm in the dro

p,
I'm
feelin'
gucci

Stay with the glock and a lil uzi
I see a opp, I act a foolie
Hit em up
Bang, bang, bang, bang
Hit em up
(Music Fades)

   The tinted window came rolling down a inch at a time. Cashmere did not hesitate to reach behind his back and clutch his pistol. His eyes turned to murder. Adrenaline rushed through him to the point he felt numb. He licked his lips in a non-seductive way. Meanwhile, the driver is the prostitute he was talking to, just a few days ago. She burst out laughing, rolling the window all the way down, so that Cashmere could see her beautiful brown face. Her slick back ponytail accentuated her features. Today she's dressed as a normal human being. And not someone's punching bag or sugar baby.

Relaxing his trigger finger, Cashmere brought his hands in sight. He wasn't in the mood for drive by pranks. He leaned against the metal pole. His hands buried in his jean pocket. The prostitute stepped out of her car, walking around to the pavement. She leaned back on the passenger side door, folding her arms across her waist.

"You're so paranoid." She smirked. "But cute."

Cashmere just stood there, observing his surroundings.

"Anyways," says the call girl. "I'm A'nessa." She pulled at her ponytail, swinging it over her shoulder.

"Cashmere Jean." He replied, overlooking her at the corner, where he saw his mother get knocked out by some guy. The words *"go away Cashmere, I don't want you seeing me this way"* played over in his head. Her blood stains were left for him to never forget. A'nessa wondered what Cashmere was looking at. His eyes were talking. She looked up one end of the street. No one was there.

A'nessa seen hurt plenty of times. By the look in Cashmere's eyes, he was feeling some kind of way. A'nessa reached for his hand, pulling him into a hug. It was a simple gesture of kindness. Her arms were soft, yet thick. The smell of her perfume soothed Cashmere more than he expected. Their friendly encounter came to an end. Cashmere pulled himself away from her. BEEP, BEEP! BEEP, BEEP! His pager sounded off. Big Lo's name slid across the small screen. Right then, Cashmere's eyes got big. A knot formed in his stomach. Suddenly, he felt nauseous.

"Are you okay?" A'nessa arched her eyebrows.

"Nah. Catch you later." He said, running toward his grandmother's house.

INT. The Alley

The last fifteen hours seemed to have disappeared in front of Cashmere. He began feeling like he himself was fading away. And the void in his heart. The deep memories in his head of his grandmother were the worst. His body shook as he ran up the alley to the back of the house.
Heart pounding so hard against his ribcage, the pressure of his pulse throbbing in his veins. Stopping at the gate of the backyard, Cashmere breathed heavily to catch his breath, panting to gain control. Slowly but surely the cramp in his side flowed away. His heart sank to the pit of stomach as he twisted the gold knob.

CONTIN...

Cashmere tried his best to keep calm, but his eyes met the broken picture frames on the floor that hadn't been cleaned up yet. Crooked pictures hanging on the wall stared back at him as he walked upstairs to his bedroom. The air is sound free of voices. Other than Cashmere's footsteps everything is quiet. He skips the stairs until he gets to his bedroom. His bed hadn't been touched, or so he thought. He checked the part of the mattress, where he stashed the cocaine, it was gone. The anger in Cashmere's eyes was just the beginning. He collapsed on the edge of his bed, resting his head in the palm of his hand. BEEP, BEEP! BEEP, BEEP!! Cashmere ignored his pager. His mother stole the cocaine. And he was going to have to find a way to pay Big Lo and Maggie back.

INT. Big Lo Comes In

His Timberland boots should have alerted Cashmere that he wasn't in the house alone. Big Lo made sure his footsteps were as quiet as could be as he crept up the stairs, a glock 19 in his hand. He gets to the bedroom, Cashmere is still sitting there. Everything is quiet until he feels the cold barrell of the flock pressed against the temple of his head.

"You're ducking my page." Said, Big Lo. "I should kill you."

He cocks the glock back. "You got the coke?"

He punished Cashmere by pressing the pistol further into his temple. Cashmere tapped his foot on the floor a mile a second. Realizing he didn't like feeling intimidated, he kept silent. Which scared Big Lo from shooting him in the face. It was the kind of day, Cashmere just didn't give a fuck. Big Lo asked him again for the second time.

"Do you have my money lil nigga?" His teeth ground together in Cashmere's ear.

"My momma took it. I don't know where she's at."

The veins in his hands began to rise up. His pupils are widening out of anger. Between Big Lo threatening him and his mother robbing him of the cocaine, he kept his words short. Big Lo however, continued on making threats at Cashmere.

"You have to pay me back." He gritted his teeth. "Maggie to." He says.
Cashmere had enough.

"Nigga." He spat. "I know what I gotta' do."

He yelled, staring up at Big Lo's three hundred pound frame.

"And fuck Maggie."

He proclaimed in a less dramatic tone.

"Bitch ain't nothing but an ass naked crack whore anyway." He sighed. "Fuck outta here." He murmured.

Big Lo wouldn't dare admit it. Cashmere had him intimidated. The careless and menacing look on Cashmere's face read, he was far from in the mood to give a fuck about anything or anybody.

INT. 1:10am- Adina Finds Cashmere

Combing the winter street of Kedzie Avenue, Adina knew of one place Cashmere may be. Coldness surrounded her as she walked the block by herself. The thought of Cashmere's warm body against hers brought a smile to her face. She pulled her cozy, cream colored gloves further up her wrists to keep them from freezing. Her matching ear muffs did justice as well. Although her ears were as red as cherries. Adina got to the corner of where Cashmere might be. Which was his house, located in the middle of the block. She observed the scenery. Caution tape is everywhere. Orange cones are in the way of anyone being able to walk through them.

CONTIN...

Adina's precise movement up the alley was well thought out. She remained focused until she reached her destination. It's so dark, even the branches on the trees were out of sight. Her heart beats faster as she twists the knob to the back door. It opens in silence. The dark room felt like a horror movie, a place where something or someone may jump out at you. Adina paced through the house using her hands to lead her to finding Cashmere. In no time, she found the staircase. On her way up there's shapes of monochrome in different colors. She gazed at the darkness, hoping she'd see the light. As she made it to the top of the stairwell, she breathed in a stench of urine.

Her own throw up nearly choked her. She covered her nose, walking slowly, feeling on the walls. One foot in front of the other, she walked her way into Cashmere's bedroom.

Since the lights were already off, she didn't bother turning them on. If Cashmere was there, which Adina felt he was. The lights would be on if he wanted them to be. Adina stopped in the middle of the floor.
(Toilet Flushing)

Her eyes widened out of fear. She moved slower than a caterpillar itself looking for a weapon to protect herself. She grabbed Cashmere's lamp off of the nightstand. She kept quiet as a mouse. The smell of her body mist perfume lingered. Cashmere returned from the bathroom to a sweet aroma. He cut the light off and on telling the truth to his eyes. That glimpse of Adina made his heart flutter.

"What are you doing here?" He appealed to know coming closer to her.

His breathing in the form of a painted picture of them on the beach.
Responding to the sound of his handsome voice, Adina answered back.

"I knew I'd find you here."

Her voice seemed to crack before getting her words out.

Furthermore, Adina loved the amusement of touching Cashmere's body. His face, his stomach.
Locking her hands inside of his, kissing him. Her neck kisses ignited something deep within him. Each time she laid her lips on his skin, he adored her more and more. The lamp fell from her hands to the floor. Nothing but darkness between them. They still felt each other's presence. Cashmere slid his hands around to Adina's

lower back. He gripped her by the waist, raising her leg around him. Adina bit his top lip. She pulled her shirt over head, revealing her c cup breasts. Skin to skin on one another, Cashmere carried Adina over to his bed. Their tongues collide together, hands all over each other's bodies. Even in the darkness of the room, the sculpture of Adina's face appeared ever so sweetly. She got Cashmere out of his boxers. Her stomach is full of butterflies. She felt his shaft against her vagina. Raising her legs up over his shoulders, Cashmere can't resist the vulnerable look he knows is in Adina's eyes. In the semi-dark, he stares at her from the lining of her lips to her belly button.

A chunk of her breast spilled out of her bra.
  Cashmere tore it off, sucking both of her nipples.
  "Shit."
  Adina gasped, pulling him into her trap of seductive kisses. Cashmere grabbed his shaft, it's rock hard. He put the head in first. Adina's tiny hands were clenched to the pillow. Next came the big boy, Cashmere thrust himself inside of her. He growled in a raspy voice.
  "Goddamn." He recited, groaning. "I'm never leaving this pussy alone."

Adina's hair is tangled up in between Cashmere's fingers. He has the touch of God. Her breasts, the same as her African American ancestors, full, and soft. Each time Cashmere put his mouth on one of them, her body reacted to him in the most intimate way. He slowly stroked her kitty from left to right. Her eyes rolled to the back of her head. Their body chemistry is so good, she slapped him on the ass.
  "I wanna' have your baby Cashmere."

She pronounced, caressing his cheek giving herself to him.

"Shit."

He murmured, kissing her.

He laid on his back, dick in the air.

"Come sit on my face."

Adina crawled on her knees toward him until her pussy was smack dead in his face. She scooted upward. The warmth of Cashmere's tongue sent lightning right through her. He clasped onto her buttocks. His mouth did the rest. Adina swore to God she had to pee. Her breathing got heavier and heavier. Her face fell into the palm of her hands. The arch in her back is evidence. Cashmere was eating her out real good. Adina's body jerked back and forth. She gawked Cashmere in the eye as he nibbled on her clitoral area. The picture of her body painted the room a pretty brown. Her figure can be seen as perfect in a place with no lights on. Music came out of her mouth. Jelly would soon flow from her vagina. Cashmere kept it up, eating her pussy until she came on his face and lips.

Chapter #14

EXT. 9pm- Kedzie Avenue

Every prostitute and their momma was on the block tonight. They pranced up to geriatric men in their skimpy clothes. Cigarettes hanging from their mouths. The only thing straight were the wigs on their heads. Big body cars were parked in the middle of the street. Their high beams on. Cashmere and Adina turned the corner. Their eyes blinded by the lights and a cloud of weed smoke. Between the beer smell and black n milds, Adina felt herself getting nauseous. Her heart burned at the taste of drugs and alcohol going down her throat. She rubbed her hand across her chest, stopping to catch her breath.

"You aight pie?" Cashmere asked.

Adina folded her arms across her belly. "I'm fine."

Cashmere didn't think twice about what was going on. He needed to make a pit stop at the spot. He prayed on the way there that Maggie would front him some more cocaine. They got to the house. There's this weird look on Adina's face.

"Babe." She says, "Why are we stopping here?"

The outside looked like someplace, she didn't want to be. She stood behind Cashmere shivering, hands around his waist while he knocked on the door. Per usual Matthias cracked the door open. The shotgun in his hand is locked and loaded. Cashmere stared into Matthias's one pupil. It's as unpleasant as a hunter during hunting season. Cashmere knows the drill from his first visit with Big Lo. Seeing how he showed up announced and with Adina, Matthias didn't let them in easily.

Cashmere turned his back toward the door, facing the street. A muted orange Subaru came to an abrupt stop. He observed the vehicle in sight. The brown male driving the 2019 whip cared nothing about being out in the open. He turned the music up louder, striking to be seen. When A'nessa got out of the back seat, Cashmere's heart sank to the pit of his stomach. As fine as she is, he

couldn't help but wonder why she was on Kedzie Avenue tricking.
(Door Opens)
　A'nessa was closing the passenger door. As she stepped onto the pavement in her red high heels, she watched Cashmere examining her. There was no way to hide being under his nose. She viewed a friend of hers coming in her direction. Cashmere's gaze on her lasted longer than what Adina would have liked to see. She mushed him right upside his head.
　"Tuh." She rolled her eyes. "Do you see me standing here?"
Cashmere on the other hand beheld Matthias waiting on him to enter the house. Adina followed behind him in complete serenity.
(Indistinct Chatter)

INT. The Trap House

　Matthias shut and locked the door, chaining the locks back together. Caothere launched his way toward the kitchen to have an engagement with Maggie. Other than the naked women all around him, Cashmere had no other problems. He propped his foot up on the wall and stood still. Adina stayed close to him. She surveyed women weighing pieces of cocaine on a scale. A few others were in the dining room counting money. The green bills flew through a money machine automatically displaying numbers in red. All of the women were butt ass naked. Adina felt scrutinized. And she was nowhere near bare in one's birthday suit. Her stomach ached as the cigarette smell filled her lungs. She felt as though she was going to vomit. But didn't want to ask to use the bathroom. She twiddled her fingers, gaping at Cashmere.

Stark-naked, Maggie came into the kitchen.
"I see you're back."
She broadcasted her provocative tone of voice.
"Guess you can say that." Cashmere reputed, barely enticing her.

He came for the drugs, that's it. He neglected everything else happening around him. Even though he knew Adina would be upset with him afterwards, he was going to take her home and come back to the block later.

EXT. On The Way Home- Adina Has An Attitude

Sleet erected out of the murky clouds, sticking to the cement of the sidewalk. Adina walked ahead of Cashmere in a blackout. Her secrecy is loud and clear, she was not in the mood to talk to him. It's cold outside. Being in a warm house would be much better than ignoring Cashmere. Across the street, two men can be heard arguing.

"This my block nigga." Says the tall dark skinned man standing on the curb.

"Nigga."

The guy argued back, sitting in the driver seat of his Buick.
"Everybody in Chicago knows, this is the money making block." "Oh yea." He pulls out a pistol.

(Gunshots)

Adina cut the corner in peace, hurrying to get home. Tears welled up in her eyes within seconds of her getting around the corner. Suddenly she felt like someone choked the life out of her. The taunting sound of gunshots rang in her head. The cold weather is invisible now. Cashmere grabbed her, comforting her with a hug. He stared into her acorn shaded brown colored eyes. He wondered what brown meant. Because her eyes are like Autumn leaves on the floor of a forest.

Spellbound by his effort to make her feel safe, Adina hugged Cashmere back. Soon after, they raced to get out of the bad weather.

INT. Home- 9:35pm- Draya Simone and Marco

(Laughing)

There seemed to be a lot of giggling and weed smoke coming from Adina's apartment. She put the key in the door, turning the knob toward her right. Her face lit up with a surprising smile. She hadn't seen her friend Draya Simone in a grip. And it appeared her and Marco were getting along just fine without her and Cashmere present. Draya smirked, dragging Adina by the arm. They went into Adina's room, shutting the door.
"Aye."
Marco says, laughing. "That's a bad lil shawty."
Cashmere tossed the diaper bag in Marco's lap. Then sat down on the sofa next to him. He patrolled Marco's actions as he unzipped the baby's bag. Maggie blessed Cashmere with twenty eight grams of pure cocaine. The crystalline flakes sparkled before Marco's happy eyes.   "Yeah boy." He nodded his head. "Bruh." He inquired. "Did you taste it to see how good the shit is?"
"Nah. I know it's good."
Crack is what had Cashmere's mammy disappearing in the middle of the night for weeks at a time. He passed on doing any of it. He'd rather get money off it than to be walking around looking like a zombie all the time. While the girl's were away in Adina's room catching up with each

other, Cashmere took advantage of cutting the cocaine into pieces.

"We need a scale or some shit bruh."
Marco pulled a pocket sized one out of his Jean jacket. Cashmere chuckled. Marco giggled just as hard.

"Nigga you just got scales on deck huh?"
"Scales on deck nigga. That's what I do."
(Laughing)

INT. Adina's Bedroom

Slowly but surely Adina was growing up fast, raising herself. She didn't have her mother knocking on doors, forcing her to go home. A place she didn't want to be when her father was around. The moment her mother walked out, she knew then, her adolescent years were coming to an end. All she had to fall back on was Cashmere's promise to never let anything happen to her. The shy look on her face made her smile.

Draya grinned.
"Your ass is blushing." She sat up on one hand. "Bitch you pregnant?"

The movie star look on Adina's face is flawless. Not only was she confident in herself. Her bone structure is elegant. Her skin is like silk over a fresh coat of paint. She laid on her left side, stretched across her bed in a turquoise crop top and ripped jeans. Her orange turban tied in a knot just above her eyebrows. She played with the button on her jeans, smiling ear to ear. Draya didn't have to wait for an answer to her question. Adina made it obvious with the way she blushed.

"Only thing I want to know," Draya giggled. "Can I be the god mom or the aunty."

"Earlier, he was checking for some girl on the Ave?"
"But is she having his baby?" Draya burst out laughing.
"I'm going to tell him." Adina smiled. "First I'm gonna take a shower."
While Adina went to freshen up, Draya let herself out to the living room.

INT. Draya- Cashmere- Marco

Out of the twenty eight grams of sneeze, Cashmere and Marco weighed each piece at fifty dollars per bag. Cashmere was getting weird vibes, like Marco was going to snort a line of the white pearl, he didn't. But it sure as hell felt like he would. The smoke and flame of the weed Marco has lit takes attention to the room.
   Draya walked clear into a bubble of fog. Her thighs capture Marco's thinking process. She appeared before him as slowly as the sun going down on a summer night. She swung her bangs over her eyes and sat next to Marco on the couch. She crossed her thick thighs over each other, caressing Marco's chin hairs. He turned to her, kissed her cheek and passed her the blunt.
(Inaudible Chatter)
Draya nodded her head, inhaling the stench of the weed. Not once did she blink as she exhaled the smoke from her lips. There's a gloss in her eyes. She enjoyed the excitement of getting to know Marco better. She wasn't oblivious to his lifestyle either, it only made her desire him more.

Chapter #15

INT. Night- Living room- 11:36pm

Cashmere pocketed the last few bags of cocaine. He stood to his feet, pulling his hood over his head. He walked toward the kitchen to wash the residue off of his hands. There were no paper towels. Cashmere examined the neglected items that kitchens needed. Things like, sponges, dish soap and brillo pads. He made a mental note to pick up some things from the store. Including a new coffee table. It wasn't all that firm on its legs. He stood in one place for a brief second, visualizing how to do the apartment over. He had a select thought on what Adina may like. He headed toward her bedroom to check in before him and Marco hit the Ave.

CONTIN...

When Cashmere opened the door to Adina's bedroom, she was standing there almost naked. A white criss cross belly top covered some of her skin. But not all of it. Her bikini cut panties stopped right below her waistline. She was retying her scarf in the mirror, when she got a glimpse of Cashmere staring at her from behind. His footsteps were as light as wind. He walked toward her, his arms came out of nowhere tightening around her waist. The aroma of his natural fragrance smelled fresh.
  Adina gazed in the mirror. The chaotic thoughts in her head of her parents not being in her life melted away. She held Cashmere by the hands, rubbing them over her belly. She had plans on telling him about her pregnancy suspicions. The words just wouldn't come out. Instead, she wound up moaning at her reflection in the mirror.

Cashmere teased her tender pussy with his fingers. Under his eye every part of her body is beautiful. Especially her facial expressions. His hands made her look at him in a way he couldn't explain. He whispered in her ear.

"You love me?"

Without hesitation, Adina shook her head yes. Her thighs are moist. She faced Cashmere, planting a kiss on the tip of his nose. She hopped up on the dresser, spreading her legs apart.
Cashmere clenched onto her, resting his head on top of hers.

"What kind of house do you want?" He asked.

His question came off sincere. From the expression on his face and affection he's showing, Adina can tell he's deep in thought. They both are. As the seconds go by, Adina becomes obsessed with her and Cashmere's relationship. Their talks weren't just words here and there. It's the silence, when they are both thinking at the same time. The light in their eyes, when one knows what the other is feeling. Adina grabbed Cashmere's hands. She put them close to her stomach. Together, they rubbed her belly. Adina leaned forward, kissing Cashmere on the lips. He ran his hands around to her lower back. The blushing look on her face complimented her eyes.

"I want a house with a red door."

Cashmere inhaled the peppermint smell of Adina's breath. He let out a cheeky laugh in her ear.
His soft hands brushing against her bost.

It was the perfect time for Adina to tell Cashmere, she may be pregnant. That moment was interrupted with a knock on the door. And Marco's voice on the other side of it.

Chapter #16

EXT. 2:06am- Kedzie Ave

Fiends crowded the block searching for their next high. Their look of uncertainty of where they'd get their dose of that good snowflake had them going crazy. They were packed on the sidewalk like a bunch of mice. A foot of snow up to their ankles. They didn't care about the cold. Nor did they fear getting frost bitten. That sugar was all that mattered to them.
  "These junkies will do anything to get high." Said, Marco, puffing on a beautifully rolled blunt.

CONTIN...

A'nessa came strutting up the street in a black mink coat. Fishnet tights hugged her thighs. A mini burgundy skirt tight around her waist showing off her curves. The pimps loved her. Out of all the prostitutes on the Ave, pimps admired A'nessa for her witty ways and stylish clothes. She never pressed men to sleep with her. In fact, she has some of them on speed dial for whatever she wants. She calls and they answer. On her way to join her circle of call girls, Faith stopped her begging for drugs.
  "I don't have anything for you Faith." A'nessa retorted. "Wait for, you know who." She said. "He'll hook you up."

Cashmere gawked at A'nessa from across the street. Although she's nothing in the world like Adina, he liked her friendliness. She didn't strike him as a washed up brainless female. Marco tapped Cashmere on the arm exhaling smoke.

"Chu' got going on in ya' head bruh?"

"What makes you think I'm thinking?" Cashmere inquired about his right hand man's concern.

"Chu' mean?" Marco laughed. "You zoned out my boy." Cashmere ran his finger across his chin. He slouched forward resting his elbows on his knees. "I think Adina's pregnant bruh."

There's a look of worry on his face. Fifteen and a baby on the way, Cashmere wasn't expecting that. He could see himself marrying Adina. Having a child hit different.

"Bruh." Marco jokes, laughing. "Yo' ass don't need to be out here then. Take yo' to the mini market and get some pampers." He cackled.

"Yea." Cashmere replied, dryly at first. "I know." He laughs.

He looked ahead. A'nessa was coming toward him. She walked through the snow as if the cold meant nothing to her.

"Hi." She smiled.

Cashmere totally disregarded her. His eyes are far away from her. His focus is on, keeping his eyes on the fiends. A'nessa glared over her shoulder. The junkie was staring at her with a worn down high. She sucked her teeth and rolled her eyes with an attitude.

"I know you're holding something." She folds her arms across her chest.

"Nope."

Cashmere answered, fibbing, wishing she'd leave.

"Give it to me." She announced, looking back. "I'll give it to her."

Marco agreed to walk with A'nessa across the street to retrieve one hundred dollars from Faith. He got the money with no problem. He slipped two bags of snow into Faith's back pocket.

EXT. Alexis- 2:30am

Alexis came stumbling out of some abandoned house higher than two junkies put together. This time around Cashmere didn't race to be by her side. He sat in the same position on the porch wondering what she was going to do in the next second or so. She was as unsteady as the tooth hanging from her gums. Alexis glanced at the ground, fumbling to her hands and knees.

CONTIN...

A dark blue Dodge Journey pulls up. Renzo swerved in the middle of the block, parking. He let his window down, plucking the ashes off of his blunt. The ashes barely hit the concrete before being swept away by the wind. Renzo inhaled another long drag. He smiled devilishly at the prospect of tying Alexis up and throwing her in the trunk. His words are raspy and soft spoken.
He'd much rather manhandle Alexis.
Alessandro pumped Renzo's breaks.
"Be gentle." He said, in his Italian
accent.

Renzo gave off the last cloud of smoke. He put the blunt out in the ashtray and stepped out of the truck dressed in all white. His size ten boots are permanently engraved in the snow. He skipped onto the sidewalk where Alexis strived to get back on her feet. He bent down slowly, stroking her cheek.
 "You want some crack." He licked his lips.

"I got some crack for you mami."

Alexis squirmed to her knees, chewing the last of the skin on her nail beds. Renzo supported her in standing up on both of her feet. He opened the door for her.
   "No. No." She pleaded, fighting him. "I don't want to go."
   Renzo shoved Alexis in the car and closed the door. Snot ran down her nose. The coldness hadn't hit her until she was actually sitting in the wagon. She sniffled, wiping her snotty nose using the palm of her hand.

EXT. A glimpse of her face- Cashmere chases the car on Kedzie Avenue

The back passenger window came down mid-way. A brown face arose from the mystic vehicle.
As long as Cashmere could remember, his grandmother had a memorable face.   "NaNa." He whispered, loudly.

Cashmere escalated his speed in which he sprawled off of the porch steps, running toward the automobile. Renzo sped off before Cashmere got to the car. Cashmere fetched his pistol from his hip.
(Gunshots)
Each gunshot reminded Elliana of the time Essence took her last breath. The bullets that shattered the windshield were tasteless.
   Renzo is driving over the speed limit, the bullets made coin dropping sounds on the concrete. Alessandro held the handle as his body jerked side to side. Cashmere's aim was to kill, grazing Alessandro's cheek.
   "Fanculo." He spat in Italian. "Fuck."

The shots kept coming. A bullet entered Renzo's shoulder. It was a bloody mess. Adrenaline so high, and lit off of a laced blunt, Renzo stepped on the gas pedal even harder. Alexis slid from her side, crashing into her mother. Elliana's fragile bones couldn't take anymore swerving. She grabbed onto her daughter for life. Having a natural body odor. Alexis began to weep. "Mama." She whispered, noticing her mother's fine brown complexion. "You're kidnapping me?" She stuttered.

"What the fuck is going on?"

A million questions ran through Alexis's mind. Her heart raced as Renzo sped over every pot hole on Kedzie Avenue.

INT. Adina and Draya- 2:56am

The breath in Adina's lungs tightened. Her ears strained to keep away the sound. Gunshots whispered throughout her apartment. She's running toward the door. But feels like she went nowhere. Draya pulled Adina by her arm. She's persuading her not to leave the house. Adina is screaming to the top of her lungs. Her eyes are soaking wet.

"Draya." She yelped. "Get off of me."

The agony in Adina's voice, the pain on her face. She could hardly stand up straight. She just knew Cashmere had been shot by one of the ten bullets. Draya observed Adina's eyes as she stared at the door waiting for a police officer to knock and tell her that Cashmere was dead on arrival. Adina's cries echoed in Draya's head. She squeezed her friend against her chest. "They'll be here." She promised. "Okay." Draya spoke softly. "I love you bitch." There was something in the way Adina sobbed. And Draya heard it.

Chapter #17

EXT. Cashmere- A'nessa- Marco

The last thing A'nessa wanted to be was a witness. She rushed to her car to get away from Cashmere and Marco. They hunted after her until they caught up to her. She wasn't that brisk, functioning in heels. Still, she didn't slow down. At that point, Marco shot his gun in her direction. Those sounds immediately caused her eyes to water and work harder at getting away from them. She landed at the driver side of her car, playing around in her Steve Madison bag for her car keys.
  "Shit." She uttered, tears streaming down her face. Cashmere grabbed her, yoking her up against the window. Her back hitting the glass made a thumping sound.
  "Who was in that car?" The grating of Cashmere's teeth made A'nessa's skin crawl. She became tense at the way he was acting toward her, just a few days ago he was friendly. Now she's stuck in his grip.
(Gun clicks)
Marco put the barrel of his Beretta against A'nessa's temple.
  "Who was in that car A'nessa?" Cashmere questioned. "Don't make me ask again."
  This time his voice wasn't as nice. His grip is tight on her. His body pressed against her torso. A'nessa squealed Alessandro's name through thick tears and clenched jaws. Cashmere and Marco both look at each other.
(Silence)

CONTIN...

Cashmere sat in the passenger seat in a daze. The idea of him seeing his grandmother's face brought an immense amount of anger in him. He eyeballed each light turning red to yellow, green and back to yellow again. The thumping in his chest made it heavy for him to keep a serene mindset. He hollered at A'nessa for slowing up at a green light. She grasped the steering wheel. Tears rolling down her face. The red light beamed against the windshield. A'nessa broke out of quietness in a raspy voice.

"Renzo and them don't play." She sobbed. "Alessandro will have him murder you."   "Who the fuck is Renzo?" Marco asked, pressing his pistol to the back of her head.

A'nessa gaped at Cashmere, hoping he'd changed his mind.

"Keep," his voice cracked, "driving."

A'nessa put her foot on the gas. They drove in silence for half a block. During the ride,
Cashmere tells Marco, he's hitting the blunt that he's rolling up in the back seat. Marco burst out laughing and said, no. He licked the blunt wrapper making sure there were no holes. He used the light off of his pager to check it.

Cashmere glared over his shoulder. "Nigga. I said, I'm hitting the blunt. I'm hitting the blunt." He says, annoyed. Marco lit the blunt. He took a long pull inhaling as much smoke as he possibly could.

"And I said," Marco exhaled. "No nigga. You don't smoke." Cashmere caught a contact off the weed Marco smoked. He wanted some to ease his mind. The plant that got Marco high was always as good as it smelled. Cashmere leaned back in his seat taking in the smoke. After a few more minutes, he peered over his shoulder.

Marco is still hitting the blunt. Cashmere howled at him from the front seat.

"Nigga go head." Marco sucked his teeth. "You're not hitting my blunt. NaNa find out she gone kick yo' ass nigga and mine for giving it to you."

The pair got into a heated fist fight. It was nowhere near personal. Cashmere's frustration built up over the last few weeks. Marco also dealt with his own issues of his mother serving a life sentence. They cussed each other aiming at each other's faces and head.

"Stop." A'nessa screamed while driving. "Let him hit the blunt one time." She yells. "Damn."

"Bitch." Marco barked back. "Hell no."

A'nessa beat her foot on the breaks. "Nigga, you can get out and walk." She abruptly stopped. "Yea alight." Marco lit his blunt again.

Cashmere kept quiet. All he could call to mind was seeing his grandmother's face.

INT. The Club- 3:27am- The Truth Comes Out

Alessandro was furious with Elliana. He'd sent instructions with Renzo on what he wanted. And expected it to be done, no questions asked.

Luckily for Renzo, the bullet didn't do much damage. He sat in a chair while one of Alessandro's workers cleaned his wound. The solution stung his skin causing him to howl. After a few seconds the sedative kicked in. He got stitched up in a matter of minutes. He stayed seated in the metal chair, shirtless. Alexis is blindfolded across from him. Her hands, mouth and feet bound to a wooden chair in duct tape.

"Umm." She murmured. "Umm. Umm. Ummph." She squirmed.

Elliana cut the tape freeing her daughter's eyes of all concealment. As soon as Alexis gained her vision back, she burst into a bawl of tears. She glanced at her mother in the twilight of a meager, isolated room. A blubber of water still cascaded from her eyes.

A few feet away from where Alexis sat was a mini bar filled with booze. She read each of the bottle names in her head. Especially the Campari, it appealed to her by the colours. Mixed in fruits and herbs, the Campari brightened up the room more than the people who were in it. Alexis craved the taste of it. In the divine moment such as this one she wasn't expecting to leave the club alive.

Alessandro walked toward the bar. He placed two glass cups on the counter. Two ice cubes clink together sinking to the bottom of each mug. In the dusk room, the ice shined. Alessandro untied a golden ribbon that was wrapped around the pretty jug. He popped the urn open pouring himself a drink.

"That's Campari." He buzzed, smiling.
Spewing another drink into the second glass vessel, he puts a lemon in the drink and a straw. He held the magic potion in his masculine hands. There's no hint in his walk that says, he didn't have a third leg in his pants.

"Italians love," he murmured, "Campari." He says, walking over to Alexis.

"In Italy," he gave a stump. "Women love this drink as much as they love anything." His accent has the tune of a guitar. "Cars, fancy clothes, Michael Khor purses." He laughs. The words rolled off of his tongue like a foreign melody. Although the demeanor of his presence is mysteriously, scary.

INT. Making A Scene- 4am

A'nessa spotted her favorite bartender. She walks up to the bar blushing at the sight of her friend.
  "Hey girl. Can you call Alessandro?" She peers at Cashmere and Marco's faces. "Tell him it's an emergency."
  "A'nessa," says the bartender.
  "Call that motha' fucka' now." Cashmere growled.

His eyes were not nice. The rage he felt, it was enough to shoot up the whole lounge. He stalked the bartender as she dialed Alessandro's number on the phone near the ice cooler. Under his supervision, she nodded her head, twirling the phone cord around her fingers. The wait was on. It was almost four o'clock. Alessandro still hadn't come out yet. Cashmere rubbed his hands together. He went back to the bar. The girl who made the call thirty minutes ago left. Another young female in a black mini skirt was there. Her back is turned, she's organizing the liquor bottles on the shelf. Cashmere jumped over the counter. The gun that was tucked on his hip is now in his hand. He pressed the barrel of it against the girl's lower back.
  She spun around.
  "You can't--" She froze, letting go of the wine bottle in her hand.
  "Shut up."
Cashmere drilled her. He pushed her toward the phone, demanding her to call Alessandro again or else he'd put a bullet in her.
  "Pick up that fuckin' phone." He urged. "Tell Alessandro to get his monkey ass up here."   The poor girl was so scared, she trembled pushing the

buttons on the keypad. *(Marco In The Background Laughing)* Alessandro yelled into the phone.
"What!"
"Your." The girl stammered. "Your daughter…"
Marco's eyes nearly popped out of his sockets. He stirred the pot, adding fuel to the fire "My bruva' gone kill yo' ass." He cracked up laughing.

Cashmere swung his feet over the counter. He slammed A'nessa back against the pool table so hard, her head hit the eight ball. He plunged his pistol in the back of her throat. Veins bulge from his forehead and neck.

A'nessa wheezed like a hungry toddler.
"Oomph oomph."

Alessandro cleared his throat.
"Please." He calmly asked, buttoning the jacket to his suit. "Take your gun out of my daughter's mouth."
A'nessa dived right into her father's arms. "Daddy." She wept.
Alessandro made it known there was a sign of stress in his eyes. The mood in the room changed. He put the soft side that he felt for his daughter on the back burner. He snapped his fingers. Guns were drawn instantly. A wide cigar hung from his bottom lip. He blew out a trail of smoke that danced upward toward the ceiling above them.

"Sorry sir." Cashmere maintained his posture. "I just--" he croaked, turning his back for a split second. The anger in his eyes is his only shield of protection. He switched from a killer to being cold and emotional.

"I just want my grandmuva' back." He raised his gun at Alessandro. His eyes said everything that he couldn't. "Where is she?"

Every one of Alessandro's worker's are moving around. But the sound of them is quiet. Big homie in the Burgundy suit cocked his gun back. The faucet dripped in the sink. No one is saying anything. Not one word. Alessandro raised one of his eyebrows and smirks, holding A'nessa close to him. Locked in one hand is his weapon fully loaded. Bullets were millimeters away from both Cashmere and Marco.

Alessandro got up to leave. He's walking arm in arm with his daughter by his side. They were inches away from leaving to send A'nessa home in a separate car, when Cashmere fired two shots in her lower back. The noise echoed throughout the room. A'nessa's shoes clacked together as she hit the walnut floor gasping for air. She squirmed in one position. Every movement her body made she screamed, crying in agony. Oxygen was being torn away from her quickly. Alessandro grabbed his daughter in his arms. Time ticked much faster than he wanted it to. Everything in the room seemed like it was going in the same slow circles. He raised his arm to put a bullet in Cashmere's chest. He couldn't pull the trigger. He couldn't let go of his daughter just yet.
(Fall On Me Playing In The Background)

I cannot see straight. Cashmere steps over A'nessa's dead body in a wave of mixed emotions. Still he feels no remorse for the loss of her life. His footsteps are as slow as a snail catching up to a turtle. He nodded at Marco to follow him toward the door ahead of them. All the while her father's eyes are overflowing with sadness. Alessandro cried in a river hanging onto his daughter's body. *I've been here too long and I don't want to wait for it*

Fly like a cannonball, straight to my soul
Tear me to pieces
And make me feel whole

Marco blew smoke from between his lips. He glanced at Alessandro one time. The door closed behind them. They didn't know the secret passages to the downstairs part of the club. It had to be one of the rooms that was down there. They walked down a short corridor that led to a sharp right turn. That turned out to be a dead end. Cashmere's heart began to race. He grew impatient every second of the way.

"Where are you NaNa?" He questioned himself beneath his breath.

It felt as though something was attached to Cashmere's back. He glared over his shoulder at Alessandro standing in front of him. All three men made eye contact with each other. Especially Cashmere! He looked deep into Alessandro's eyes. His soul was gone. One move could determine the rest of Cashmere's life. And if Alessandro decided to kill him, he'd never get the experience of being a father to him and Adina's baby. They rise some feet away from each other. Alessandro is smeared in his daughter's blood.

"Twenty five years," He says, rubbing his chin. "I've been in the drug business." His feet glide forward on the floor.

"Nobody ever," he emphasized, "Took anything that belongs to me." His voice made the corridor feel dreary and unsafe. He pulled his gun from his hip. "Tonight, you took something very special from me." He whispers, choking on his words. "So now," he says, "I'm going to take something from you."

Marco clutched the trigger on his missile. Meanwhile, Cashmere had a reason for his actions. It became easier and easier for him to put a rocket in someone's body. He exhibited his feelings toward Alessandro.

"With all do respect sir." Cashmere breathed. "You took something from me too." He sneered. "Where is she?" He uttered, drawing his sword at the infamous Italian mob boss.
(Alessandro laughing)
"You stop at nothing, I see."

Chapter #18

EXT. Early morning

Cops responded to the shooting on Kedzie Ave. Of course it was the famous Finley and his partner Williams. They sat in their police vehicle on the corner of the ave waiting on witnesses to show themselves. In Chicago that didn't happen often. The pair opened their doors at the same time. Their husky boots imprinted in the snow. They pulled their skullys over their heads to keep the wind off of them. Black leather gloves kept their hands warm. The cold breeze, however, stung their cheeks as they approached the first house in front of them. Williams pounded on the door three times. BANG! BANG! BANG!
   Finley observed the area for any other witnesses that may have known what happened. He gaped over his shoulder at the empty street. All that was visible was the tire marks left behind. He jogged down the stairs finding shell casings in the middle of the road. He picked it up. "Look what we have here." He turned to Williams.

INT. The Club- All Hell Breaks Loose

Alessandro led Cashmere and Marco through a grand chamber full of expensive, Italian art. Two seated rose coloured sofas graced the zone of the apartment like area. It was simply gallant for a man like Alessandro.

   Marco read the likeness of A'nessa's mask that hung in a sumptuous, halcyon frame overlooking her father's mahogany workspace.

   Cashmere hiked past the print. He kept some feet away from Alessandro. They reached a five foot, Teal coloured sliding door.

   Cashmere gulped, swallowing the saliva in his mouth. On the reverse side of the exit was a staircase leading downstairs to another dark place. The intuition in Cashmere's stomach told him this is where his grandmother was. He braced himself to kill anything and anybody who seemed to be moving or acting funny and shady. The trio treaded down the steps. There was little to no radiation flashing back at them. Their tracks raised the hairs on everybody's backs who sat in suspicion.

Renzo gaped over his shoulder. He raised his arm pointing his gun at the unknown people coming out of the darkness of a low sunrise. When he realized it was Alessandro, he settled down. The two men shook hands.
(Indistinct Chatter)
All four of their footsteps were gradual as if they were skating on frozen ice. The music of depression filled the room.
Cashmere believed his eyes. There was no doubt in his mind. Not even for a second. It felt like he couldn't get to his grandmother fast enough. Her brown skin is the map to her soul. It was then Cashmere discovered who his grandmother really was. He collapsed into her arms. One arm around her neck. The other hand holding his pistol. Cashmere gave Alessandro one of the most evil eyes anyone could see. He looks at his mother and his feelings

are everywhere. Part of him wanted to care. His mind said one thing. But his heart was saying something totally different.

Alexis uttered the words, "I'm sorry son." One last time.
((Fall On Me Playing In The Background)

A fearless look came over Renzo's face. He held the gun tight around the surface of the trigger. He squeezed it three times. The force of each bullet knocked Alexis sideways. She hit the cold floor. *THUMP!!* Her head bounced off of the canvas. The bullets left her body weak and stiff.

Blood gushing at a rapid flow soaking her hands and chest.

Cashmere walked over to his mother's body. He knelt down beside her to shut her eyes.
(Marco Sniffling)

Alessandro whispered something in Renzo's ear. By the look of his face, it wasn't over. More blood was going to be shed. Renzo disappeared for a quick minute. When he returned, he had a cop with him. The same cop from that night at the subway. Renzo shoved him forward.

"Keep walking motha' fucka." He said, pressing the butt of his gun against the cop's head.   "This is my favorite part." Alessandro laughed. "You steal from me." He points at himself. "I kill you." He uttered, shrugging his broad shoulders.

He studied the cop's face as Renzo put him on a stool, tying a rope around his neck.
Alessandro stood in front of him.

"Where is my cocaine?" He asked. "Where is my money?"

"I have it." Cashmere answered. "I was there when..."

"Bruh what the fuck are you doing?" Marco spoke in Cashmere's ear. "Nigga you tryna get us killed or some shit?"

"We gotta make a deal with this motha' fucka." Cashmere's teeth grinded against each other.

"They will kill NaNa if we don't." Marco sighed.

"Exactly nigga."

Marco spoke his piece to Alessandro, curious to know how much the cocaine was worth. Him and Cashmere agreed to push the product on Kedzie Avenue only if his grandmother was kept alive.

Chapter #19

INT. 5am

The uber ride on the way home was as dreadful as Cashmere seeing his mother gunned down to her last breath. It was much better to have found his grandmother untouched and with all of her limbs. She held Cashmere's hand, while sobbing on Marco's shoulder.

"I," she stuttered. "Wish your grandfather was--" The tears streamed from her eyes. "Here." She wept. The hurt on her face would be there for a long time. "A house is not a home without him." She burst out crying on Marco's chest.

Cashmere wedged his and Elliana's hands together. A thousand questions swormed in his mind. There were no clues that he could think of about his grandmother's secret lifestyle. To his memory, she ran a tight ship and nothing less.

The uber came to a stop.

"You know shawty gone flip on you." Marco said.

"Yea." Cashmere replied in a raspy voice. "I know."

CONTIN...

Adina had just dozed off after waiting up all night for Cashmere to come home. Her tender eyes were exhausted. She'd been throwing up half the morning feeling sick to her stomach. She slept comfortably in her bed in a deep snooze. Her hand lay across her belly. One leg stretched out underneath her ugg blanket. When Cashmere turned the knob to go into her bedroom she was dreaming out cold.

Cashmere tiptoed toward the bed turning on the lamp. His hands appeared on Adina's body. Soon his lips were on her neck. In an instant Adina's eyes fluttered open. Cashmere's kisses never change. They just get more seductive than the last one. She pushed him away from her. "I'm not being nobody's second option Cashmere." Adina tossed to her side.

"Never that. Why are you trippin on me like this Adina?" Cashmere asked, crawling up beside her.

"Because I'm pregnant." Adina blurted out. "And I don't wanna lose you." She hysterically cried.
Cashmere squeezed Adina close to him.

"Look at me." He said, caressing her cheek. She turned toward him. "I found my NaNa."   "Alive?"

"Yea." Cashmere retorted, relieved. "It's all over."
"And your mom?"
"She's dead." He replied, gaping over his shoulder.

Cashmere sat up facing the wall. He wasn't expecting Adina to ask about his mother. Truth be told, he wanted to forget the images in his head. It was like a horrible dream that he couldn't wake up from. In that moment he felt so gone. Adina wrapped him up in her arms. She had a hug stronger than anybody Cashmere has ever known. In her presence, time stood still. Cashmere's head sagged in her lap. She kissed his forehead. Tears rolling down both their faces.

Chapter #20 Ten Years Later

INT. Clarendon Hills- 7pm- Summer Time

Business in the hills ran great. Cashmere made enough money over the last ten years to buy Adina a house like he promised her twenty five years ago. Their ten year old son C.j wanted for nothing. They made sure to give him a child star life. As long as he went to school everyday and got good grades, he pretty much earned whatever he wanted. Speaking of the young god, C.j came running in the house.
 Adina stopped him at the stairs.
 "C.j." She said.
 "Sorry ma." He giggled. C.j went out of the front door and walked back in like he knew how.   "But ma." He said, showing Adina the smudge on the bottom of his red K-swiss sneakers. "I got some dirt on my kicks."
(Adina laughing)
 C.j grew to be a grandma's boy. Before going to the guest bathroom to clean his shoes, he went to the dining room where Elliana sat knitting to give her a big juicy kiss on the cheek. At ninety five years old, she smiled every time she saw C.j's handsome, copper coloured face.
 "I love you NaNi." He called her.

INT. Cashmere- Marco- 8:30pm- Rudy's Bar & Grill

 "Aye bruh." Says, Marco. "Draya is pregnant."

"Your goofy ass waited all damn day to tell me, I'm going to be an uncle." Cashmere jokes.
(Marco Laughing)
"Can a brother share his good news over proper drinks?"

The shot of Patron disappeared from his glass. He swallowed the sweet drink ordering another round on his tab. Cashmere glanced at the time on his Rolex watch.
"Let's finish this celebration at the house with the wifey's." He suggested. "Adina's making her famous pasta tonight." He says, putting a tip on the counter.
"Bet
. I'll pick Draya up and meet you over there."
They drowned their second drinks and parted ways.

CONTIN...

Cashmere pulled up beside Adina's rose pink Chevrolet Malibu. He shut the engine to the car off. Thinking back over the last decade, he took a moment to appreciate the home Adina made into a house for their family. Especially for his grandmother. He admired Adina for that everyday.

EXT. Time Up

Draya was sitting at her vanity, brushing her hair into a ponytail.
(Phone Rings)

Like I Want You
She answered Marco's FaceTime call on the second ring, putting her IPhone down to finish her hair. They discussed dinner at Cashmere and Adina's house. Of course Draya

agreed to go over there. She blew Marco kisses through the phone.

"Draya." Marco smiled, flashing his gold teeth. "How many of my kids are you going to have?" Draya blushed, holding the brush in her hand. "As many as you want me to." She laughed.

"Babe I want a quickie." She bit her lip.

"That's why yo' ass pregnant now." Marco cackled. "You always want the D."

"Shut up babe." She giggled. "I love you Marco."

Coming up on a red light, Marco stopped, holding his foot on the brake pedal. The reflection from the light shined through the phone. Draya saw that Marco was sitting at a red light.

"I'm almost home baby. I love you too." He said.

A car passing in another direction of Marco's car fired six bullets, shattering the windshield. Marco's face crumbled in pieces, falling forward against the steering wheel. His chest caved in from the impact of pressure that hit his body. His car swerved in the middle of the street, crashing into a parked car. Edges of the broken glass were covered in Marco's blood. "Marco." Draya screamed. "Marco baby answer me." She collapsed to the floor. "*Pleease.*" She howled. "Please. Please. Please." She sobbed.

CONTIN...

In the midst of Draya's breakdown, Adina called. Draya clicked over.

"Sis."

She squealed.

"Draya." Adina's voice trembled. "Sweetie what's wrong?"

"It's Marco." Draya whispered, through all of her tears. "He got shot sis." Adina's heart nearly burst out of her chest.

"Mommy are you okay?" C.j asked.

Adina grabbed C.j by the hand. She didn't do well keeping her tears in her eyes. They escaped her eyes one at a time. She wiped her cheeks.

"I want you to go to the window and see if your father's car is outside. Can you do that?" Just as C.j peeked out of the window, Cashmere came strolling in.

"Yo. Yo." He laid his keys on the table. "Babe I'm home." C.j came running toward his father. "Sup dad."

"What's good son. Where's your mom?"

"I'm right here."

Adina came out of the guest bathroom in a ball of tears.

"It's Marco babe." She stuttered, walking toward him. "He's dead." Cashmere scoffed.

"Nah. Nah. Nah." He said. "I was just with him babe. Chu' talkin bout?"

"Babe." Adina glared in his eyes. "He's gone."

Water welled up in Cashmere's eyes. The pretty vase on the table, he picked it up throwing it against the wall. "That's my fuckin' brother. That's my brother." He paced the floor until his knees grew weak.

"Daddy." C.j murmured. "Did uncle Marco die?"
(Phone Ringing)

Adina reached for the phone. Suddenly red and blue lights surrounded her house. THUMP! THUMP! THUMP! Finley and Williams banged on the door. A swat team of their colleagues in bullet proof vests swarmed on the front lawn with guns in their hands. Adina grabbed C.j and ran to the dining room.
 "Mommy I'm scared."
 "I know baby." Adina sniffles. "Can you be a big boy and make sure NaNi doesn't get hurt?"
(Gunshot Sounds)
 All over again the depressing sounds reminded Adina of Kedzie Avenue. She shoved C.j underneath the dining room table. Scurrying to her feet, she wheeled Elliana into the guest bathroom.
(Glass Shattering)

Elliana's face dropped. Her cheeks sunk inward. Chunks of tears streamed down her face as she held onto the blanket she was knitting. She looked at Adina. Her fragile eyes aching. "I won't let anything to him." Adina pants, out of breath, referring to Cashmere. "I promise."
 Adina raced to the attic as fast as she could. She put the combination into the safe where
Cashmere kept all of their weapons. She snatched the clip off of the wall of the safe, loading it with bullets. Adina slammed the lockbox shut. She sprawled down the steps to Cashmere sitting on the floor. His knees are up to his chin. His hands are entwined in one another.

Adina bent down beside him. Her body moved at the speed of a snail. She buried her head in the nape of his neck. Lights are flashing throughout the house.

"Don't make this any harder than it already is Cashmere Jean." Cashmere heard Finley yell, outside of the door. "Come out with your hands up." He yelped.

Williams nodded his head at the swat team as a signal to bust the door in. "I'm giving you until the count of three." He howled, aiming his Beretta at the door.

Adina stood to her feet. She put her back against the door, cocking the clip to the Uzi back. She projects her voice enough for Finley to hear her.

"My eleven year old son is in here." She wept. "I'll open the door." She says, "Drop your weapons."

Adina swiped the tears from her eyes, gawking at Cashmere, who's in a distraught zone. He's looking at Adina, but emotionally, he doesn't see her. Swat officers ran to the back of the house, toting their shields as protection. The sheriff's helicopter dwindled above the house making noise.

EXT. Swat Team- Finley- Williams

Finley whistled for his colleagues to stand down. They looked at him as if he'd lost his goddamn mind. Their department had been after Cashmere and Marco since they were teenagers. Williams barked at Finley, questioning his orders. Finley's eyes lit up as the lights circled Cashmere and Adina's residence.

INT. Coming Out

Options were limited. Adina nor Cashmere could run. Adina cracked the door in a slow gesture. As soon as one of the officers saw her face, he raised his gun to put her down. She slammed the door shut, screaming.

"Finley." She cried hysterically. "Anything happens to my husband or my son." She squeezed her eyelids together. Yet the tears flowed back to back. "I'll fucking kill you." She uttered.

She laid eyes on Cashmere. "What do you want to do babe?"

"There's nothing to do." He answered dryly. "My brother's dead." He looks up at Adina.
"Marco's dead."

"I'll walk out with you." Adina said, crawling in Cashmere's lap. "Whatever happens, happens." Her voice cracked. "It's me and you baby." She played with his chin hairs. "It's me and you til the bloody end."
(Red and Blue Lights Flashing)

CONTIN...

The swat team had made their way inside of the house without making a sound. They stayed light on their feet as they got closer to the living room. A tall white man designed in prison tattoos nodded for his colleagues to check the dining room. Obeying the command, the officer located C.j hiding underneath the table. He put his glove over C.j's mouth to keep him from yelling. He carried C.j outside while the other's finished the job.

"C.j." Adina whispered out loud. "Baby are you okay?" There's no answer from him. Adina stepped away from guarding her home. She walked into the swat team coming at her. They bombarded her, rushing to lift Cashmere off of his feet, just as she hurried past them running toward the dining room to get C.j.

"Get up motha fucka."
They gripped Cashmere up by the collar of his suit. The tattooed cop swung the door open. On the way out, he read Cashmere his rights.

"Cashmere Jean." He said. "You're under arrest for drug trafficking, extortion, pimping and money laundering. Anything you say, can and will be held against you in the court of law."

As they're walking out of the front door the cops smile as if they'd hit the lottery. The flickering red and blue lights mock the darkened street of Cashmere and Adina's home. In those lights Cashmere's silhouette complexion shined bright. His feet glide through the glass leaving permanent footprints. High beams blind the officers.

Draya pulled up in her black SUV. She ran toward Cashmere. She's tugging at him, crying. Meanwhile, Adina is wrestling to get C.j out of the officer's arms. She snatched her son from the cop's grip. She pushed him behind her. Her hand came flying across the cop's face. He reached for his taser. His colleague tapped his arm notifying him to let it go. Adina sped over to Cashmere.
(Slow Motion)
"I love you forever." She kissed his lips.
Cashmere held eye contact with
C.j. He glanced back at Adina.
"Take care of my son." He said.

The two women fell into each other's arms. Draya cried on Adina's shoulder in the palm of her hand and the tears cascaded down her face, sliding through the cracks of her fingers. She sank to the ground not caring whether or not her Fashion Nova sweatsuit got dirt on it. Emotions swirled around in their head. They held onto each other figuring out what to do next.

Chapter #21 Five Years Prior

INT. The Plan

"You're alive because of your grandmother." Said, Finley to Cashmere. "Don't ever forget that."   He measured the pool stick on the purple ball, shooting his shot.
   "But cha' boy Marco is a hot head."
   He sits on the corner of the table. "Always has been."

Cashmere raised an eyebrow, staring at both Finley and Paco. He loosened his tie out of frustration. The annoyance on his face showing how he felt. He grabbed his pool stick, sharpening the tip of it. He leaned forward focusing on what ball he wanted to knock off of the table. He glides the stick between his fingers, hitting the yellow ball. A waitress in a sheer black mini skirt and heels stopped by the table bringing Cashmere a shot of Patron. He winked at her for the beverage getting back to the conversation he and Finley were having.   "Tuh." Finley scoffed. "You and ya' boy think you can't be touched."
"You said so yourself." Cashmere sarcastically replied.

He tossed the pool stick on the table. There was nothing to see except his back as he vanished outside of his grandmother's establishment.

CONTIN...

Finley knew all too well that a day would come where Marco would rat him out. Even if it meant taking a bullet for Cashmere. Word leaked that Finley and a handful of his colleagues have been dirty cop's for years. Afraid that Marco was going to testify against him in court, Finley put a contract on Marco's head for two million dollars.

"We can't kill Cashmere." Paco said. "That's for damn certain."
"Then kill his brother." Finley smiled devilishly.

Chapter #22

INT. Six Months Later- River City Correctional Center- 8:53pm

One hand on his stomach the other behind his head, Cashmere stared up at the grey ceiling. A thousand memories of Marco flooded his memories. The worst of it all was remembering his reaction when he told him Adina might be pregnant. Which she was. Marco was ecstatic to be an uncle. The first week of C.j being born, Marco went out and dropped a bag on a twenty four karat gold necklace with C.j's initials engraved in it. He also got him a custom diamond piggy bank made with the word boss on it.

Cashmere tossed and turned all night long. Missing Marco's funeral turned him into an evil individual. He felt like he betrayed Marco. The night rewinded in his head over and over again. Every time he closed his eyes, he saw Marco's face. Falling asleep wasn't as easy as it once was.

The cot Cashmere laid on is thin as paper. There's no support for his back. The springs constantly poked him in the ribs. Almost every other night, he woke up with a Charlie horse in his leg and a crook in his neck.

The worst was yet to come. In six minutes the lights were going out. Cory, the C.O on duty came by Cashmere's cell. A young white male with dark brown hair to his shoulders and blue eyes.

"You want anything boss?" He gripped the bars, staring through them at Cashmere.

"Yea, boss." Cashmere hollered. "I want my fucking brother back." He beat his fists against his chest. His eyes bulge from his sockets. He spun around in a circle. "I want my fucking brother back." He lost his voice, smacking the roll of tissue onto the floor.
(Cashmere Sniffling)

His backside met the concrete wall as he slid downward, hitting the floor. Four white walls were closed in on him. There was nothing else to do except daydream while looking at them. Cory cleared his throat. He'd never been in Cashmere's shoes, so he couldn't relate to the way he felt. He sighed heavily.

"I'm sorry bruh." He uttered.
Cashmere gapes up at him.
"The fuck away from my cell." He uttered.

The lights flickered until they shut off and Cashmere's box became a black hole. A drip of water splashed in the dingy sink. In the gloom, Cashmere couldn't forget that he was trapped inside of four walls. His stomach grumbled for a hot meal. Preferably Adina's cooking. That wouldn't happen any time soon. Especially having a fifteen and a half year sentence.

INT. 9:36am- Saturday

The ceiling in Cashmere's cell had become his way of escaping his thoughts. He often laid on his back in the same position everyday of the week. He'd trained his mind to not think or eat the disgusting food that the prison cooked. His stomach gripped quite often. Majority of the time, he felt nauseous. Dehydration caused him to lose that smoothe brown look. His cheeks hung low. The structure of his jaw seemed out of place. His ribs weren't showing, just yet. In due time they would be.

As much of an asshole Cashmere was to Cory, his mother always taught him to be kind no matter what. She believed acts of kindness were the medicine to anything. Cory came walking down the d-block where Cashmere's cell was. In his hand was a Dunkin Donuts bag and a medium cup of hot, lightly roasted coffee. Cory hid the bag and the coffee behind his back. He leaned up against the metal bars. For a minute, he stood there watching Cashmere stare up at the ceiling. The smell of fresh ground coffee beans turned Cashmere's attention to see where the aroma was coming from. When he examined Cory standing there, Cory grinned. His eyes lightened up.
  "I thought you'd never look over here." He said, smiling with his eyes. "Don't tell nobody." He checked to the rear of him making sure no other C.O's were present. "This is between you and me." He slid the bag of food and coffee through the cracks of the metal bars.
  "Enjoy." Said, Cory.
Cashmere sprinted up to his feet. He dragged himself to the bars.
  "Why are you doing this?" He asked, holding eye contact. "The man find out you slippin niggas--"

"I don't see you as that man." Cory shrugged. "I was raised to see people not color." His eyes fluttered, gaping at Cashmere waiting for him to say something.

Cory snuck off before the other inmates woke up. Cashmere glanced at the bag. Whatever was in it, smelled delicious. He mustered up the strength to bend over and pick the bag up off of the floor. He slithered over to his cot in the jail slippers that were given to him. When he opened the bag, there was a bacon, egg and cheese bagel wrapped in aluminum. Cashmere's stomach growled at the sight of the juicy sandwich. He lifted the top bun up. It's toasted just right. Cashmere bit into the sandwich. Butter drips down his wrists as he's chewing. He's taken away by the deliciousness of the food. After swallowing each bite, he enjoyed a sip of his coffee. His throat was soothed by the warmth of the drink.
(Footsteps Approaching)

A C.O shoved his key into the hole, unlocking Cashmere's cell. He slaps the coffee out of Cashmere's hand. He raised Cashmere to his feet, pushing him back against the wall. His eyes are mean and hateful.

"Who brought you that food motha' fucka?" He spat, through clenched teeth. Spit flying from his lips. "Was it Cory?"

Cashmere didn't speak one word back. He let his weight fall on the C.O's hands. They examined one another in the eyes. There was chewed up bacon in Cashmere's mouth. He swooshed it around spitting pieces of food in the C.O's face.

"I ain't no snitch motha' fucka." Cashmere slurred, laying his head against the wall.

The C.O cleaned the grease particles from his face, wiping his forehead with the palm of his hand. He cackled beneath his breath. Cashmere's wool, curly hair became tangled up in the C.O's firm grip. The C.O lunged forward kneeing Cashmere in the stomach.
   "Spit food in my face motha' fucka." He says, tackling Cashmere onto his cot.
   Cashmere wanted to kill that C.O instead he head butted him busting his nose. He rolled over to the floor holding his stomach. The breakfast came up in chunks like a running faucet of water. Tiny pieces of bacon got caught in his throat. He coughed it up laying face down on the floor.
(Panting)
   Prison was a nightmare for Cashmere. And with Marco gone he just couldn't figure out his life anymore.

CONTIN... 10:09pm

Word got back to a group of red neck guards, working the graveyard shift. They were going to make an example out of Cory. Mauslowski, a blonde haired man and a bald spot in the middle of his head came to Cashmere's gate. He cackles, unlocking it.
   Cashmere had fallen into somewhat of a coma. For the first time in months, sleep felt good. His dreams were just beginning. In his trance, he pictured Adina's lips on him. She had the most adorable kisses. After each one, she rests her chin on his shoulder, smiling. "I love you." She'd say, stroking the line of his jawbone.
   Reliving family times, Cashmere heard the sound of C.j's footsteps running toward him. He giggles beneath his breath.
(C.j's Voice Echoing)
   "I'm going to be just like you when I grow up dad."

"Nah son, son. Be better than me aiight."

Cashmere felt his breathing getting heavier. His eyes are soaking wet. All of a sudden the police bust through the door, yelling with their guns out. "Get on the floor. Get on the floor now." Cop lights flash against Cashmere's skin. They wrestle him to the floor. C.j looks at his father. Cashmere glares back at him. Waking up before the cops could arrest him, the chills of the handcuffs stayed on Cashmere's wrists. His eyes are halfway open. He saw the guard standing over him. But thought nothing of it until he gripped him up, dragging him to a dark room. When they reached their destination, the guard turned on the light. Five white men in their uniforms were sitting in folding chairs.

Two of them were leaning against the wall. None of them seemed nice or like they cared for colored folks. Cashmere cared nothing about the police or how they felt. He locked eyes with Cory, who, the guards, had standing on a metal chair. A rope restrained him around the neck. And his hands are bound in duct tape. The guard sitting down stood to his feet with a set of clippers in his hand. He gives them to Cashmere.

"Go on boy." He says, smacking on tobacco. "Give em a good cut." The brown spit from his mouth hits the floor.

Cory spoke through his bloody lips. "Do it." He said, squinting his swollen eyes open.

Cashmere breathed lightly. The guard yoked him up threatening him to obey orders or else he'd be on a chair next to Cory. The guard chuckles in Cashmere's face.

"Inmates aren't allowed to have outside food." Said, the short chubby guard. "Did Mr. Noakes sneak you food?"

Mauslowski chewed his gum, spitting it out at Cashmere's feet. Cory looks at Cashmere. He nods for Cashmere to say yes, it was him.

"I told you motha' fucka--" The cuss word rolled off of Cashmere's tongue in the most disrespectful way. He dropped the clippers on the floor. "I ain't no snitch."

Cory's head fell to his chest. He knew after tonight, he'd never get to tell his mother he loved her. And for teaching him respect and love. Mauslowski kicked the chair from under Cory's feet. They beat him until he turned purple. The chubby guard held Cashmere's hands behind his back, while another forced his eyes to watch Cory's slow death.

"Tell my mom, I love her." Cory uttered. "Tell her, I love her more than life itself." Cashmere wanted to close his eyes. He couldn't. The guard's fingers were imprinted in his face, tearing some of the skin from the crease of his eye.

"You talk about this to anyone." Said, Mauslowski. "I'll find ya' wife and kid," he smirked. "And
I'll kill em. I'll lynch their black asses right in my backyard. And toss them in the river."
Mauslowski patted Cashmere on the shoulder. "Chubs." He gapes at the heavier guard. "Clean this shit up. Meet me on C-block when you're done."

Mauslowski carried Cashmere back to his room. He pushed him inside, locking him in there until morning.

Chapter #23 Six Years Later

INT. December- 3pm

Inmates didn't know the names of visitors coming to see them. Normally guards called their names and escorted them to where the phones were. Mauslowski tightened his hand around Cashmere's wrist as they walked to a separate part of the prison. Mauslowski unleashed Cashmere from his handcuffs. A sly look is on his red face. Cashmere walked straight toward the telephone booth. He pulled the chair out and sat down. Although he didn't see anyone right away, he sat there. His head fell into the palm of his hands.

It was then Paco came out of the shadows. He picked up the phone, speaking at a distance. Had Cashmere heard Paco's voice, then saw him, he would not have believed it was him on the phone. Cashmere picked up the phone. His skin felt like it was melting. His heart pounded in his chest. After years of no contact, he didn't know what to say. Paco started out speaking low.   "I just wanted to say, I'm sorry man." The words hardly came out of his mouth. It damn sure was written all over his face.

"Speak up bruh." Cashmere told him. "I can't hear you." His voice echoed through the phone.   "It was me." Paco stuttered. "I killed Marco."

Cashmere's vision became blurry. His eyes began to well up with tears. Everything around him started to look fuzzy. Then he saw nothing at all. His consciousness drifted through sounds of static. His heart beat so loud, it echoed in his ears. The feeling in Cashmere's body slowly left until his mind was pitch black.

He jumped out of the chair, smashing the phone against the glass, howling, "I'm going to kill you motha' fucka."

He repeatedly bashed the phone against the window. The phone fell from Paco's hands. As he's getting up to leave, Adina comes in with C.j. She saw the anger on

Cashmere's face. It was a hurt she'd never seen before not even when his grandmother went missing.

Adina pulled C.j close to her. On the way out, Paco slaps him on the arm and keeps walking. Meanwhile the guards have Cashmere restrained. There was a time Paco protected him and Marco. He would speak and they were attentive. It was his voice of gold. Yet in the storm of the situation, Paco became a grim cloud to Cashmere. The soul in his eyes vanishes as the guards drag him away from the phone booth. Adina's banging her fists against the window. Her arms feel like spaghetti.

(Footsteps

Approaching

)

A guard slid up behind her.

(Indistinct Chatter)

INT. The Hole- 4:46am

Mourning had become Cashmere's day and night time song. His mind forever goes back to the days he was a free man and Marco was alive. The memories were just as bad as having nightmares.

INT. Three days later- 5am

Asad Afreen began his morning saying the Fajr prayer. He raised his hands to his ears.
   "Allahu Akbar."
The tone of his voice resonated into thin air. His masculine chest is guarded by his smooth hands. He gawks at the floor.
   "A'auodu billaahi minash-shaAllanir rajeem."
He breathes inward with great focus, reciting the opening chapter of the Qur'an.
   "Bismillaahir ar-Rahmani ar-Raheem
Al hamdu lillaahi rabbil 'alameen
Ar-Rahmani ar-Raheem
Maaliki yawmid deen
Iyyaaka na'aboodu wa iyyaaka nasta'een
Ihdeenas siraatal mustaqeem
Siraatal ladheena an 'amta' alayhim
Ghayril maghduubi' alayhim waladawleen

   As he's bowing down to the ruku position, he says, "Allahu Akbar." Asad keeps his back straightened out. His hands are pressed on his knees. And his almond eyes are to the ground.
   "Subhanna rabbeeyal adheem." He says, three times.
   Rising up from ruku, Asad came back to a standing position. He brings his hands to his ears.
   "Samee allahu leeman hameeda."

Standing upright, Asad lowered his hands to his waistline. "Rabbana walakal hamd. Our Lord, to you is all praise." He muttered.
   Bowing to the sujud, Asad's knees are to the area rug beneath him. As well as his hands. His forehead came to a slope. The spine of his back straight. Asad performed the Sujud for five seconds.
(Silence)

CONTIN...

The strange words rang in Cashmere's ears. He'd never heard anything like it, but it soothed his raging spirit. Cashmere got up from his cot, staggering to see who and what the noise was. When he glared out between the bars, Asad had just raised to his feet. There's an instant connection between him and Cashmere. Their eyes meet. Asad was like a reincarnated version of Cashmere's older self. Cashmere saw himself clear as day in Asad's reflection. Asad smiled through his eyes.
   Time stood by their side. And for the next nine years, Asad dedicated himself to teaching Cashmere the lifestyle of becoming a muslim.

INT. The Last Day- 11:52am- Spring

Asad and Cashmere trade stares at one another. They come face to face in the yard, greeting each other with much respect. The smile on their faces expressed a tremendous amount of love and gratitude. Asad took a white cloth from his shoulder. He wiped the perspiration from Cashmere's forehead.

"Cashmere Jean." Mauslowski called out. He hawked spit on the ground. "Time to go boy." Cashmere looks back at Mauslowski. Asad smirked.

"Be safe out there, my brother." He grips Cashmere's hand. "Ashan Ashar." He said, meaning the one with wisdom and the most beautiful.

"Allahu Akbar." Cashmere said, thankfully.
Their brotherly hug spoke of a deep procision. Nine years of discipline brought both men extreme wisdom and clarification of who, they chose to be for the rest of their lives.

The world stood still for a second as Cashmere walked toward his freedom. Asad called Cashmere's name. "Ashan Ashar." He came to him.

In his hand was a set of white cloths and a hijab. The white custom jalabiyyah robe came sealed in a clear bag. Cashmere greatly accepted Asad's gift to him. Although Asad was sentenced to life. He and Cashmere would continue to communicate via mail.

Chapter #24

EXT. 1:32pm

Shrouded in a printed dress with baby blue flowers on it, Draya complimented her outfit wearing a jean vest and a pair of pink Converse sneakers. Gold hoops dangled from her ears. On her right arm, she wore Marco's diamond watch. Her hair is brushed up into a sock bun. She hadn't aged that much. However, her eyes were still sore from losing the love of her life. While waiting for Cashmere to come out, she sat in her brand new silk white Suburban truck looking at pictures of her and Marco. The same as it was the first day of his death, the tears flowed one after another.

Draya held onto the steering wheel, water soaking her cheeks. Her eyes are so full of sorrow, she never looked up to see Cashmere walking toward her. She jumps out of the driver side, running into his arms. Both their eyes glimmer in the heat of the sun.

Cashmere held Draya in place. Meanwhile she winced on his shoulder. *(Silence)*

INT. The Car Ride Home- 2:09pm

"Thanks for coming sis." Cashmere smiles, a free man. He grabbed the photo off of the dashboard. "So this is my niece huh?" He laughs.
Draya bobbed her head yes. "She has my brother's lips and nose." Cashmere flipped the picture over. He read the name out loud. "Cashmeen Jean." He glared out of the window.

Draya pulled over on the shoulder of the road. She put the truck in park. She grabbed Cashmere's hand. "Your brother wanted you to know this bond is forever." She whispers.

"I love you sis."
"I love you brother."

EXT. 4:30pm- Home sweet home

Being the spiritual person that she grew to be, Adina uplifted her husband's name everyday since the police took him away from her and C.j fifteen years ago. She sashayed through the house in a green-ish, blue silk scarf. Her v-neck shirt clung to her upper body, showing a portion of her stomach.

Her highrise, printed shorts fit perfectly around her tiny waist. She goes into the kitchen to prep for dinner. C.j had come over to help his mother cook. Today wasn't the greatest, but Adina pushed on to make a home cooked meal. The weary look on her face was lonely.

"Mom bear." Said, C.j "It's gonna be alright." He kissed her forehead.
(Adina giggles)

"You remind me of your father." She wiped the tears from beneath her eyelids. "God. I love that man." She says, stuttering in the palm of her hand.

CONTIN...

Draya came inside the house more cheerful than when she left. It was about to be a bittersweet moment for their family. A lot of tears were going to be shedding.

"Sup aunt Draya." C.j kissed her cheek.

"Sup, my handsome nephew." She smiles, laying her purse on the chair. "Where's Cashmeen?"

"Honey." Adina chuckles. "Where she always is." She says, wiping down the counter with a wet wipe. "In her uncle's bed on FaceTime talking to some lil boy."
(C.j Laughing)

"Lil ninja better keep his dick in his pants when it comes to that one."
"C.j" Adina stuck her hip out.
 C.j burst out laughing. "I'm sorry mom bear."   "Umph

hmm." She giggles.

Cashmere didn't make a sound as he crept toward the kitchen. The laughter coming from the best place in the house warmed his soul. He came from behind the wall, the gift in his hand from Asad.
   "C.J junior." Cashmere spoke.
The tears were already welling up in Adina's eyes. Adina trembled to the point, she dropped the tub of butter on the floor.
   "Pop." C.j glared at his father.
   "Yea son." Cashmere approached him. "It's me." He said. "I'm home now."
   Cashmeen jogged down the stairs. She abruptly stopped where she was at. Cashmere burst out in tears. Cashmeen had Marco's whole face in person. He squeezed her in his arms, kissing her face. "My family." He said. "My family."
   "I love you uncle Cashmere."

Adina faced the sink. Her brain stuttered, putting together the pieces that were missing all those years. In Cashmere's eyes, she saw all of their memories. They reminded her of the way he looked at her every time they made love. Cashmere comes up behind her. He gave her that hug, she loved so much. The smell of him brought more tears to her eyes. His aroma was like fresh baked acorns. Adina clasped onto him....

INT. 10pm- The Love Scene

The touch of Cashmere's hand got Adina out of her clothes. His breathing brought her everything good that she's been wanting. He reached for her face. The urge to kiss her show in his eyes. It's the feeling of being intoxicated by her love.

Adina loved that Cashmere was all man. Confident in who he was. Everything about him is peaceful. His mustache adorned his features. Adina needed Cashmere to feel the same way he did anytime they were intimate. That he wanted her and nobody else. Cashmere was close enough to Adina's face. He sucked her into a kiss she could always remember. That's when the tricks began with him using his tongue. He was all business, pulling her shorts down. Before Adina knew it, Cashmere's tongue was up in her pussy.

Her pretty, red painted toes sunk into the satin sheets. In the shadowy room their hands lock up. They're drunk in love.
Cashmere laid silhouette against Adina's thighs moving his tongue faster and faster. His perfect jawline is strong and muscular. Adina arched her back. She's panting, feeling herself getting ready to cum. In a half of a second, she oozes cream all over Cashmere's lips. She surrendered herself to him. They've waited for this moment for so long. Now that it was happening. They didn't want to stop. Twisting and turning, it started all over again.

Adina pulled Cashmere up to her. She craved for him to make love to her. And he did. All night long.

CONTIN...

Adina's nightmares seemed so real. Sleep paralysis held her on her back while tears escaped her eyes. In her coma state of mind, she's screaming at the police to let Cashmere go. The glare from the lights blind her. The sirens going off. "Get off of him." Adina yelps, in her sleep.

"Baby." Cashmere, says. "Wake up wife." He muttered.

Adina sat up in bed panting. She's holding Cashmere's hand clutching it as if he were going somewhere.

"I had a dream," she wept uncontrollably, "the cops were taking you away from me again." She sobbed.

"Sshh." Cashmere put his finger over her lips. "I'm a free man baby. I'm here."

Unsure whether it was the right time or not, Cashmere brought Adina's attention about him going to do God's work on Kedzie Avenue. She sat up quickly.

"Are you crazy babe?" She questioned him. "Kedzie Avenue is the past."

Her eyes shift toward him. Cashmere could tell, she was worried about something happening to him. He pulled her back down to lay on his chest.

"Baby I'm muslim. That means, I have to do the work of God."

"Then I'm going with you." Adina spoke in a low tone.

(Silence)

Chapter #25

INT. June 30th- Noon

Cashmere looked himself over in the mirror. His jalabiyyah garment fit him like an angel sent from the heavens above. The hair on his chin is braided neatly. He slides his manicured feet into a pair of all white flip flops. The heel of his feet are nice and smooth. His fragrance smelled of chocolate cookies.

(Knock Knock)

C.j stood in the doorway.

"Sup pop."
Cashmere grabbed the second set of garments off of the bed. His gesture was for C.j to enter the bedroom. The rhythm in which C.j walked is quite impressive to his father.
"Sup pops." C.j asked. "What's in the bag?"
"A gift I got when I was in prison." Cashmere replied. He puts the robe and turban in C.j's hand. "Put it on." He tells him.

C.j changed into the garment in the master bathroom. The lighting matched well with his chocolate skin. He placed the turban on his head. He looked exactly like his father. Accept he was the younger version. When C.j came out of the bathroom. He stretched out his arms.
"How do I look pop?"
"Like a King." Cashmere bowed to his son.
C.j wasn't sure that he should bow back, he did anyway. A smile spread across Cashmere's face. He got his Qur'an off of the nightstand and was ready to go.

As the father and son are coming down the stairwell, Cashmeen is leaning against the wall on FaceTime with her lil boo.
"Hol' up pop." Says, C.j. He whispers in Cashmeen's ear. "Tell your lil boyfriend, he try any shit. I'll cut his dick off and send it to his mammy. Ya dig." He burst out laughing. "Love you C." He kissed her cheek before leaving.

EXT. Another Tragedy

A bad feeling settled in Adina's stomach. It'd been a long time since she or Cashmere stepped foot on Kedzie Avenue. Cashmere purchased them a house in the hills and never thought to look back afterwards. The city of

Chicago never did fix the potholes that sunk deep into the ground.

Adina pressed on the brakes. Her tires dipped downward making a thumping sound. Cashmere stared out of the window at the junkies that hung around the leaning poles. He pulled at the braided piece of hair on his chin, uttering the muslim prayer for peace. "O God!" He said.   "O our master! You are eternal life and everlasting peace by your essence and attributes." There was a parking space at the corner of the stop sign.

"Pull up right there babe."

C.j observed his surroundings. It made him uncomfortable seeing extra thin women strung out on crack.

"Mom bear, this is where you and pop grew up?" He asked, disgusted.

"Right around that corner."

Adina answered, staring over her shoulder.

Cashmere tapped his fingers on the side of his thigh. He wondered if he was doing the right thing. Adina turned in her seat toward him. She kissed the back of Cashmere's hand.

"I'm proud of you husband."

The beam in her eyes put a gracious smirk on Cashmere's face.

EXT. Friendly

The three of them stepped foot outside of the car. The first person to get Cashmere's attention was a young black. He looked to be eighteen or nineteen years old. A furry black purse hung from his arm. He walked in purple stilettos up to his knees and a red wig.

Cashmere gulped, feeling sorry for the young man. He walks up behind him.

"Excuse me brother man."

He spun around in them stilettos as fast as lightning.

"Don't brother man me." He said, in a drag queen voice. "My name is Dangerous, you can call me Dutch." He paddled his wig. "And who, you is?"

Cashmere introduced himself as Ashan Ashar.

"This is my wife Adina, my son C.j." Dutch glanced at the book in Cashmere's hand. He wondered what it was. Especially since Cashmere and C.j both came on the Ave dressed like a saviours.

Cashmere interpreted the signature of the publication. He explained to Dutch that the album of the text had information in it that could change his life.

"O our sustainer." He put his hand on Dutch's shoulder. "Grant us the life of true peace and usher us into the abode of peace."

Cashmere tore a piece of paper from his notepad giving it to Dutch. "Anytime you want to talk brother."
Adina smiled at Dutch rubbing his arm.

"That wasn't so bad was it." Cashmere jokes.
(Cop Sirens)

CONTIN….

Good ol Finley and Williams sped up on the curb nearly running C.j over. Adina uttered under her breath.

"Tuh. This motha… babe you better talk to him." Adina rolls her eyes.

She pokes her hip out pouting her lips. She couldn't handle looking at Finley's face. She walked to her car, sitting in the passenger's seat. Finley on the other hand made a personal call to Alessandro making him aware of Cashmere's discharge back to society.

"Well, well, well." He sat on the hood of his car. "If it isn't street king, Cashmere Jean."   "Cute wife." Williams said, with pure sarcasm. "Beautiful robe." He tugged at C.j's garment, laughing. C.j balled his fist up jamming it in Williams mouth.

"You don't know me bruh." C.j spat.

"Yea." Finley cackled. "My partner and me--" he said, "We don't know you. In fact," he lit a cigarette. "We don't want to. You're irrelevant to us." He bust out chuckling.

Cashmere took a few steps forward, so close in Finley's face, he knew for certain he had Finley scared. Cashmere let his almighty presence do the talking for him. His eyes spoke different languages. They could easily be translated as ready for war. The dispatcher's voice came over the walkie talkie.

"You better get that." Cashmere's stern voice raised the hairs on Finley's neck.

Williams was the first one to get in the car. Finley smirked, putting his cigarette out on the hot pavement.

Dutch's pimp, Marlon had some questions for Cashmere. To be exact, he inquired about Cashmere reading parts of the Qur'an to Dutch. He shoved Cashmere back against a parked car. Cashmere fell into the car. The anger on his son's face is clear to see.

"Son." Cashmere pointed, panting through his teeth. "Go to the car. Now." He ordered.

Marlon pulled out a .22 loaded, chrome pistol.
"Nobody is going nowhere."
His gold fronts glistened in the sun. C.j looks at his father.
"You need to put that gun down, bruh."
He addressed Marlon head to head in a respectable manner. Their eyes glisten in the sun. Both gawking at each other. No fear in either of their eyes. Cashmere would have loved to introduce Marlon to a couple of bullets with his name on them. It wasn't the Muslim way. Cashmere wanted nothing but peace. He came in peace. And he intended on leaving that way as well.

Marlon lowered his arm, chuckling as if he didn't want beef. His face turned cold. The veins in his temple popped out. He squeezed the trigger three times. C.j fell backwards onto the burning cement. Blood gushed out of his garment, staining the filthy sidewalk. Dead is a place of no return. It's forever and ever.
"Uncle Marco's going to be so happy to see me." He said, his eyes rolling back.

Blood began to trickle from C.j's mouth. The light in his eyes no longer existed. He went on to a higher place. One hand over his chest. He was gone for good.
Adina heard the street sounds half way up the block. Her feet hit the ground. It felt like she was stuck. She's running down the street. But it seems as though it's taking her a lifetime to get to C.j. When Adina finally made it to her child. The heartbeat in her legs ceased. She crawled the rest of the way toward him. Glued to that moment, her hands became sticky with C.j's blood on them. Her tears came faster than she ever thought they could.

Cashmere's hands shook uncontrollably, the Qur'an fell from them. It landed on the concrete face up. He didn't notice the blood on his hands. He saw them turning pale. He held C.j against his chest, bobbing back and forth. A weeping howl worked its way out of Cashmere's mouth. The sound of him roaring moved like dark clouds on a rainy day. His face is to the sky. He's screaming, "*Nooooooo.*"

(Ambulance Sirens)
(Cop Sirens)

Adina's cries whistled out of the cracks of her teeth as the coroner laid the body bag on the ground to put her son in. The gloves on their hands protected them from direct contact with the victim's blood. They lift C.j off of the pavement. Although he's deceased. They are gentle with his body. Adina's legs are too weak for her to stand on her own. She fell to the concrete grabbing at the bag. Cashmere wrapped his arms around her. He squeezed her tight. The whisper of his voice entered her earlobe.

  "I gotchu babe. Til the bloody end." He murmured. "I got you."

THE END

Made in the USA
Columbia, SC
18 June 2024